Harvard Health Publishing
Trusted advice for a healthier life

Dear Reader,

Good for you for picking up this Special Health Report. That means you realize the importance of strength and power training—and you're doing something about it. Most people are familiar with the recommendation to get 150 minutes of moderate aerobic activity a week. But they often overlook the recommendation to do muscle-strengthening exercises two or three times a week.

Strength training offers benefits beyond big biceps or six-pack abs—payoffs that you just can't get with aerobic exercise, despite its many virtues. It is the type of exercise that will do the most to keep your muscles and bones strong as you age. Strong, powerful muscles will keep you fit, so you can enjoy your favorite activities like hiking, skiing, or gardening for longer. They'll make keeping up with your kids (or grandkids) easier. They might even help your golf or tennis game and make it easier to lose weight or stay slim.

And if you have certain health concerns, strength training may help with those issues, too. Studies show that strength training can help prevent or control conditions as varied as arthritis and diabetes. And new research shows it may also play a role in preventing some types of cancer.

While strength training is a familiar concept to most people, power training, which builds both strength and speed, may be new to you. There is overlap between the two, but think of it this way: strength training may help you lift your suitcase into the overhead bin, but power training can help you react quickly to catch a package that falls from the bin.

This report offers four strength and power routines that give you total-body, multi-muscle moves and also improve your balance. You'll begin with workouts using dumbbells and your own body weight or resistance bands. Then you can add medicine balls or kettlebells to take it to the next level. Finally, there's a section on plyometrics, or jumping exercises, that you can incorporate into any of the workouts to rev up your calorie burn and maximize muscle power.

In every workout, we offer easier and harder options, so you can adjust the workouts to your own strength and fitness level. (Note: While this program is highly adaptable, we recommend that you start with our earlier report, *Strength and Power Training for Older Adults*, if you are over 65 or have health problems such as heart disease, diabetes, or joint or bone problems.)

Whatever your age, the strength and power training routines in this report will help you look toned and feel younger and more vital. Above all, we hope you will have fun working out. We do!

Elizabeth Pegg Frates

Elizabeth Pegg Frates, M.D.
Medical Editor

Michele Stanten

Michele Stanten
Fitness Consultant

The basics: Strength training, power training, and your muscles

The last time you visited the doctor, you may have received a list of recommendations to improve your health—lose 10 pounds, reduce your salt intake, get plenty of exercise. But chances are, your doctor didn't specifically mention strength training or power training. Most people, including doctors, don't give their muscles enough thought, except maybe when they pull one. But just like your heart and brain, your muscles play a vital role in your life. And how you treat them now can make a big difference in how much fun you will have for years to come.

Strong muscles help with obvious things like unscrewing a tight lid, but they also power your golf swing or tennis serve, put spring in your dance step, and keep you going whether you're hiking up a mountain or crossing the finish line. Stronger muscles also make mundane tasks like carrying groceries and raking leaves easier. But if you neglect your muscles, you will find that these activities require more effort as you age.

In your mid-30s, you start to lose muscle mass at a rate of 1% to 2% a year, and strength decreases by 1.5% a year. That may not sound like much, but these little changes add up in your 40s and 50s and may contribute to achy joints, an increased risk of injury, and an expanding waistline. The less muscle mass you have, the fewer calories you burn throughout the day,

Strong muscles play a bigger role in your everyday activities than you may realize. And they are one of the best tools you have to keep you looking toned and feeling fit as you age.

which primes your body to gain weight.

As you reach your 60s and 70s, muscle loss accelerates to 3% a year. This can make everyday activities harder, which may cause you to become less active. The less you do, the weaker you become, so activities feel harder. Eventually, even simple tasks such as climbing stairs and getting out of a chair become more difficult. And then you do them less frequently, which contributes to more weakness. It can become a dangerous downward spiral.

However, these changes are not an inevitable part of aging. Strength and power training are some of the best tools you have to keep you looking toned and feeling young. They may even help keep your brain fit. A study of British twins (ages 43 to 73) in the journal *Gerontology* found that, among 324 twin pairs, those with the most muscle strength maintained the best performance on memory and cognitive tests over a 10-year period—and had greater brain volume on brain scans.

Before delving into all the benefits of muscle-strengthening exercise, it helps to review what strength training is, how power training is different, and how these exercises affect your muscles. In this chapter, you'll also learn how muscles work and how aging and inactivity contribute to the loss of muscle strength and power over the years.

Strength training: The traditional approach

The classic image of strength training is body builders hoisting heavy barbells. But strength training is much broader than that. Strength training is any exercise that builds muscle by harnessing resistance—that is, an opposing force that muscles have to strain against. It is also known as resistance training, progressive resistance training, weight training, or weight lifting. There are many ways to supply resistance. You can use your own body weight, free weights such as dumbbells, elasticized bands, or specialized machines. Other options include medicine balls, kettlebells, and weighted ropes.

No matter what kind of resistance you use, strength training builds muscle. This not only makes you stronger, but also increases your muscles' endurance, making activities like hiking up hillsides or carrying heavy bags easier. It will also help you to maintain a firmer physique. And it doesn't take as much work as you might think to start seeing results. Multiple studies have found that men and women who lifted weights two or three times a week gained an average of three to five pounds of lean weight (muscle) in 10 to 16 weeks. When you consider that you've probably lost that much muscle mass over the last decade—and you've been losing muscle since

Strength training—also known as weight training or resistance training—helps build muscle. Just two sessions a week for three to four months can make a real difference.

about your mid-30s—you can see how important strength training is as you age.

The benefits are not limited to your muscles. These exercises can strengthen your bones as well. When your muscles contract, they pull on the bones to which they're attached, and this force stimulates your body to reinforce the bones with added minerals. Note that the only bones that benefit are those attached to the working muscles, which is one reason why it's important to do a full-body workout that exercises all the major muscle groups. The workouts in this report will do that.

Power training: A complementary approach

Another type of training, known as power training, is proving to be just as important as traditional strength training in helping to maintain or rebuild muscles and strength—maybe even more important.

As the name suggests, power training is aimed at increasing power, which is the product of both strength and speed, reflecting how quickly you can exert force to produce the desired movement. Thus, faced with a mountain hike, you may have enough strength to reach the summit. But can you keep up with the younger members of your hiking group? Power, not just strength and cardio fitness, can get you up the steep inclines quickly and safely. By helping you react swiftly if you trip over a root or lose your balance on loose rocks, power can actually prevent falls.

To develop power, you need to add speed as you work against resistance. You can do this by performing traditional strength exercises such as push-ups or biceps curls at a faster pace, while maintaining good form. Plyometrics (jumping exercises) also build muscle power. The rapid acceleration as you leap into the air and then the rapid deceleration as you land increase your ability to produce explosive power—for example, darting across the street when a car ignores the crosswalk sign or chasing after a toddler headed for trouble. Exercises such as medicine ball throws increase upper-body power, so you're better able to catch something you've dropped (like your cellphone) before it hits the floor.

Power training may be even more important than

strength training, because muscle power declines at more than twice the rate that strength does as you age—as much as 3.5% a year for power compared with 1.5% for strength. That's why some doctors, physical therapists, and personal trainers are now combining the swift moves of power training with slower, more deliberate strength training exercises, as do the workouts in this report, to reap the benefits of both activities.

A look at muscles and movement

Any voluntary movement in the body is made possible by skeletal muscles, which are attached to bone. The body boasts more than 600 skeletal muscles that enable you to walk, twist, swing your arms, turn your head, flex your feet, wiggle your toes, and more. Figure 1 (below) shows the muscles you'll be exercising with the workouts in this report.

Some of these muscles—like the biceps and triceps in your upper arms—are muscles you've heard about your whole life. But a well-rounded strength program works major and minor muscle groups throughout your body. This is especially important if your current exercise routine is limited to some of the most popular cardio workouts like walking, running, or cycling. These activities focus on the lower body, so muscles in your upper body are often neglected. Strength training balances things out by providing a workout

Figure 1: The muscles you'll be working

For each exercise in this report, you will see a line indicating "Muscles worked." The diagram below shows where most of those muscles are located. However, there are some exceptions. Certain muscles we name in the exercises are not visible here, since they are underneath other muscles. The rhomboids are underneath the trapezius muscles in the back and link the shoulder blades to the spinal column. The erector spinae muscles run vertically along the spine. The internal obliques lie underneath the external obliques. And the psoas major and transverse abdominis lie deep beneath the lower portion of the rectus abdominis.

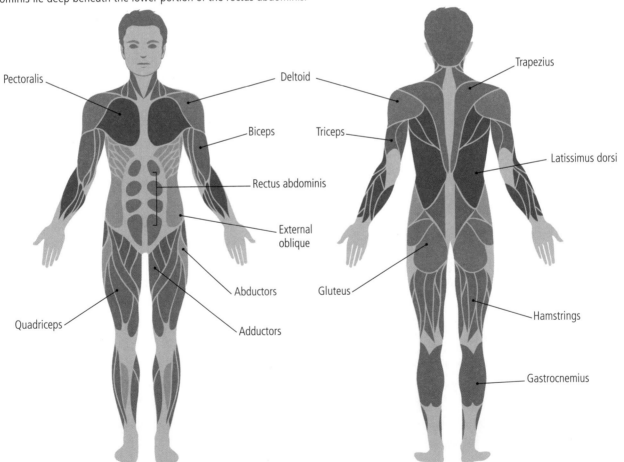

Table 1: Know your muscles

A well-rounded strength training program works all the major muscle groups. These are the major muscle groups in your body and the actions and tasks they perform. The workouts in this Special Health Report will ensure that you train all of these key muscles.

BODY PART	MUSCLE	ACTION	EXAMPLE
Shoulders and arms	Deltoid	Moves your entire arm at the shoulder joint	Waving arm overhead
	Biceps	Bends your arm at the elbow joint	Raising a glass to drink
	Triceps	Extends your arm at the elbow joint	Pushing up a window
Back	Trapezius	Moves your shoulder and shoulder blade	Shrugging
	Rhomboid	Pulls your shoulder blade back	Starting a lawnmower
	Latissimus dorsi	Pulls your arm down	Pulling down a window
	Erector spinae	Extends and stabilizes your spine	Standing tall
Front of torso	Pectoralis	Moves your arm up, down, in, and out	Pushing something away from you, lifting a child off the floor
	Rectus abdominis	Bends your torso	Sitting up in bed
	Transverse abdominis	Stabilizes lower spine and pelvis	Pulling your belly in
	Internal and external obliques	Rotate your torso	Dancing the twist
	Psoas major	Bends and rotates your leg	Marching
Hips, buttocks, and legs	Gluteus	Extends your leg behind you	Standing up from a chair
	Quadriceps	Extends your lower leg at the knee joint	Kicking a ball
	Hamstrings	Pull your heel toward your buttock	Running
	Abductors	Move your leg away from the midline of your body	Swinging your leg out to the side
	Adductors	Move your leg toward or across the midline of your body	Kicking your leg across your body
	Gastrocnemius	Point your toes	Rising up onto your toes

for the total body, including the core muscles in your abdomen and back. The core is the sturdy central link connecting your upper and lower body and, as such, assists everything from swinging a golf club to bending to pick up a package. When muscles throughout the body remain strong and balanced, you can perform at a high level with less risk of injury.

When you're young, it's easy to do tasks or play sports despite muscle imbalances, but this changes as you age—and it's never ideal, no matter how old you are. Any time you move, your muscles are applying force. To balance this force properly, different sets of muscles move in opposition to one another. So, as you walk upstairs, the quadriceps muscles on the front of your thighs act as agonists, meaning that they initiate the movement. On the back of your thighs, the ham-string muscles work as antagonists, meaning that they help to control the movement. This synergistic relationship is the reason you need to exercise both sets of muscles; otherwise, you will create an imbalance in strength that can increase your chances of being injured, especially as you get older.

For a well-functioning, injury-free body, it's also important to work some of the deeper and smaller muscles. For example, the abductor and adductor muscles in your legs and hips are vital to keeping you upright as you walk or run, so you want to keep them performing at a high level. The routines in this report involve these and other small, deep muscles along with the more superficial ones that provide nice definition. Table 1 (above) explains the functions of the different muscles that are targeted in the workouts.

Muscles in motion

As you perform the exercises in this report, your muscles will engage in three types of action. Paying attention to what your muscles are doing as you execute a move will improve your form and technique, so there's less chance of injury.

Concentric action occurs when muscles exert force and move joints while *shortening*. When people think of using their muscles, this is usually what comes to mind—for example, flexing an arm to show off the biceps muscle in the upper arm. This is the same type of motion you would use when bending your arms to lift a bag of groceries out of the back of the car or hoisting the bag up to the kitchen counter.

Eccentric action occurs when muscles exert force and move joints while *lengthening*. As you slowly lower your grocery bag, the biceps muscles lengthen while producing force, so that you lower the object in a controlled manner rather than simply letting it drop. Eccentric strength is especially important for maintaining balance, mobility, and everyday functions.

Isometric (static) action creates force, too, but muscles don't shorten or lengthen much and joints do not move. If you push against a wall, for example, or try to lift an object that is far too heavy for you, you'll feel your arm muscles tense. But since your muscles can't generate enough force to lift the object or shift the wall, they stay in their usual position instead of shortening.

Here's what all of that means in practical terms. Concentric and eccentric muscle actions create movement, whether you are lifting weights, jogging, or simply walking across a room. As you perform an exercise, the muscle targeted by that exercise will alternate between concentric and eccentric actions. For example, as you lift and lower a weight, your biceps will first shorten (concentric action), then lengthen (eccentric action). The opposing muscles, the triceps, also do both, but in the reverse order—lengthening as the biceps contract and vice versa. Because your muscles work in tandem, both muscle groups get some benefit, but the primary movers—in this case, your biceps—get the most strengthening.

Though most people tend to think of the concentric phase of the exercise as the whole point of that exercise, both phases are important. Slowing down the eccentric phase of an exercise has been shown to improve strength gains. However, you are also more likely to experience soreness a day or so after training in this manner. The strength workouts in this report use tempos that achieve maximum strength gains with minimal soreness.

As for isometric exercise, your core muscles perform this type of contraction when you are doing exercises like a lunge or a standing overhead press in order to stabilize you so you don't fall over. Isometric muscle actions result in very little movement, such as when a soldier stands at attention, but they are essential for maintaining your balance.

Muscle physiology

A muscle seems like a simple thing. But a single muscle may have from 10,000 to over a million muscle

---

Figure 2: An in-depth look at muscle

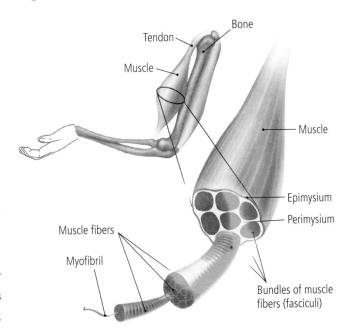

Your muscles are joined to bone by cords of tissue known as tendons and are covered in connective tissue known as the epimysium. If you could look inside your muscles, you would find that they are composed of small bundles of muscle fibers, known as fasciculi. These bundles are surrounded by connective tissue, known as the perimysium. One muscle may have anywhere from 10,000 to more than a million muscle fibers. In turn, each muscle fiber consists of hundreds to thousands of tiny, interlocking strands called myofibrils.

fibers (also known as muscle cells). Inside muscle fibers, you will find protein, glycogen (sugar), and fat stores that provide energy for muscle contraction. In order for the fibers to function together as a unit, they are grouped together in small bundles known as fasciculi (see Figure 2, page 6).

Still, muscles do not contract on their own. They rely on instructions from the brain, conveyed by nerves. A single nerve cell, or motor neuron, directs activity in a specific group of muscle fibers (a process known as neuromuscular activation). Together, this grouping of a nerve cell and its corresponding muscle fibers is called a motor unit. If a given nerve cell commands only a few muscle fibers, the motor unit marshals less force; the more fibers the nerve cell controls, the greater the force the motor unit exerts.

Within the motor unit, nerve impulses act by triggering a complex set of chemical reactions that cause contractile proteins (myofilaments) deep in the muscle to slide over each other, generating force. Movement occurs when that force ripples through the muscle structure to the tendons, which in turn tug on the bones. Essentially, the bunching muscles act like strings that make a puppet spring to life.

Strength and power training exercises push muscles to develop greater capacity. Muscles grow in response to this stimulus because the exercises increase the production of new muscle protein. When this cycle occurs repeatedly, muscles become stronger, muscle mass increases, and muscles may become visibly larger, particularly in men. Women can develop more shapely arms and legs, but they are unlikely to develop big, bulky muscles unless they spend hours a day in the gym, because their bodies have far less of the male hormone testosterone, which contributes to muscle bulk. Interestingly, even if there is no muscle growth, strength and power training enhance the nervous system's ability to activate motor units.

Slow-twitch and fast-twitch fibers

Most skeletal muscles have two main types of muscle fibers: slow-twitch and fast-twitch. Usually, a combination of the two types gets called into service when you exercise. Slow-twitch fibers function best during

Most skeletal muscles have two main types of muscle fibers—slow-twitch and fast-twitch. Generally speaking, strength training is better for developing the former, while power training favors the latter.

low-intensity activities, when they can be supplied with oxygen. These fibers can keep working for long periods of time and are called upon first for most activities, including aerobic activities such as walking, swimming, biking, or jogging.

During anaerobic activity (rapid, high-intensity exercise in which your body is unable to meet the muscles' significantly higher oxygen demands—for example, short bouts of sprinting, jumping, or scrambling up a hill), fast-twitch fibers step into the breach to create bursts of power. Generally speaking, strength training is better for developing slow-twitch fibers, while power training favors the fast-twitch fibers. But in fact, you usually use both to varying degrees when you exercise.

Studies show that functional activities—that is, activities that people do in their daily lives—also call on both kinds of fibers. Take something as mundane as washing the dishes. The slow-twitch fibers act during most of the slow-paced activity of scrubbing, rinsing, and drying. But when you reach overhead to put away a heavy dish, the fast-twitch fibers are recruited because you are doing something that needs a short but more intense burst of power.

Now that you know how your muscles work, prepare to be impressed in the next chapter by the array of health benefits strength and power training can deliver. ▼

What strength and power training can do for you

No matter how old—or how young—you are, strength and power training can offer benefits. Studies in children and young people, some as little as 8 years old, have found improvements in sports performance (among athletes), body composition (among those who are overweight or obese), and physical and psychological well-being (across all categories). And benefits continue across your life span, even into your 80s and 90s. Some research has included subjects as old as 98 and has shown that strength training helps the elderly stay independent longer.

One of the reasons that strength and power training are so potent, especially as you get older, is their ability to curb muscle loss and build new muscle. As mentioned earlier, muscle loss begins around age 35. On average, adults who don't do regular strength training can expect to lose 4 to 6 pounds of muscle per decade.

If you're trying to lose weight, that might sound appealing, but it's not a good thing. First, most people don't see the number on the scale go down because of muscle loss, since they are usually simultaneously replacing that firm, compact muscle with bigger, lumpy fat. That's why you may notice your pants feeling snug even if the scale hasn't changed. Second, muscles fuel metabolism, so the less muscle a body has, the slower its metabolism, meaning it's burning fewer calories throughout the day—exactly the opposite of what you want it to do. And if you're trying to lose weight by cutting calories,

The single most important thing you can do to maintain mobility and independence as you age is to stay active. Don't let your muscles go.

you're likely losing even more muscle over time.

Strength training can counteract this effect. According to a research review in *The Journal of Sports Medicine and Physical Fitness*, when participants dieted, on average 27% of the weight they lost was muscle. Combining dieting with cardio exercise cut muscle loss in half. But when they combined dieting and resistance training, *all* of the pounds lost were fat.

The more muscle you have and the stronger your muscles are, the more benefits you'll get, even beyond weight loss. You'll develop a slimmer, firmer figure. You'll be more active. You'll get more out of your cardio exercise because you'll be able to go faster and last longer. Strength training can even improve your golf game. After 10 weeks of training, 29 amateur female golfers (average age, 58) improved their drive speed and distance, according to a study in the journal *Physical Therapy in Sport*. In another study, power training produced even greater improvements in 20 competitive pre-elite golfers over a nine-week period.

Moreover, there are specific health benefits to strength and power training, such as better blood sugar control and a slowing of bone loss.

Given that you only need to put in an hour or so of effort every week, that's a lot of benefits. This chapter delves into more of the research on strength and power training, starting with power training, which is newer to the scene and has been studied less extensively.

© Jupiterimages | Getty Images

Health benefits of power training

Football players, high jumpers, gymnasts, tennis players, and other athletes have long used power training—particularly exercises with weighted vests or plyometrics (jumping exercises)—to help improve performance. Many studies have documented not only improvements in performance with power training, but also reductions in injuries.

For non-athletes, there aren't as many studies on power training, but research in this area is growing, especially among older adults, and it has already yielded promising results. In one study, 18 healthy older adults (average age, 71) received eight weeks of either low-intensity power training or low-intensity strength training targeting the hip adductors and abductors (see Table 1, page 5). Power training was more effective at enhancing neuromuscular activation, resulting in more strength, better coordination, improved balance, and quicker reaction time. The power-trained adults were also better able to stabilize themselves after a light push, suggesting that they may suffer fewer falls. Another study of 74-year-olds found that power training increased the participants' walking speed and stride length.

There may also be benefits for people with certain medical conditions. One small study tested three types of exercise—strength training, power training, and stretching—on people with osteoarthritis of the knee. After 12 weeks of exercise, participants in all three groups had better function and less pain, but those in the power training group registered the greatest gains in strength, power, and walking speed.

Power training can help even if you have severe joint pain. In one Danish study, 40 people who were scheduled for hip replacement surgery did power training twice a week for 10 weeks. Following their conditioning, the power trainers reported less pain and stiffness and better daily functioning, along with gains in muscle power, compared with another group of 40 patients who did no exercise. The changes were not dramatic enough for the participants to delay or cancel their joint replacements, but the researchers speculated that this level of improvement might enable people with less severe osteoarthritis to delay surgery. The power trainers not only did better before surgery,

but afterward, too. In a follow-up study, three months after surgery, those who had done power training were further along in their rehab than those who did not exercise before surgery.

Certain types of power training might also help you increase bone density by a small amount. Plyometrics are high-impact moves. The repeated pounding signals the body to strengthen bones that are experiencing the stress, so they will be better able to handle the impact. Over 16 weeks, women ages 25 to 50 increased bone density in their hips a half a percentage point by doing 10 to 20 jumps twice a day, according to a study published in the *American Journal of Health Promotion*. While that may not sound like a lot, the women who did not do jump training not only did not gain any bone density, but actually lost almost three times that amount.

Other studies show that power training can improve function and quality of life for people with multiple sclerosis or Parkinson's disease, and those who've had a stroke—three conditions that result in excessive muscle weakness and dysfunction. For example, power training helped restore some muscle movement speed that is often lost with Parkinson's disease. In people who've had strokes, power training helps with regaining walking speed. And improvements in strength and power may help reduce fatigue, a common symptom of multiple sclerosis.

Finally, it is well documented that both aerobic exercise and strength training can help improve cognitive function in older adults. Now it appears that power training may help, too. In another study, women with mild cognitive impairment who followed a 12-week program of power training showed more improvements in their mental abilities than did those following a similar strength training program. The women showed significant improvement on two tests for dementia—the Mini-Mental State Examination and the Montreal Cognitive Assessment.

Health benefits of strength training

Scientists have long known that strength training is good for you. Conditions as varied as back pain, heart disease, arthritis, osteoporosis, diabetes, obesity, and insomnia can be partly managed by strength training and other exercise regimens. But what is the relative importance of strength training versus aerobic workouts? Relatively few large, long-term studies have examined this question. Some things are clear, however.

Strong muscles never sleep. While strength training doesn't burn as many calories as the same amount of time jogging or swimming, it does appear to have a bigger afterburn. Technically called "excess post-exercise oxygen consumption," it is the extra calories you burn after an exercise session as your body returns to its normal state. Generally, the higher the intensity and the longer the workout, the longer this excess calorie burn lasts. That means the more strength training you do, the more calories you can burn even after you put the weights down. One study found that on non-exercise days following strength training, participants burned on average an extra 240 calories a day through everyday activities—a significantly higher amount than on days following cardio.

Other studies confirm that strength training can increase your metabolic rate (the rate at which your body converts energy stores to working energy) by up to 15%. This means you burn more calories, even while you're sitting or sleeping.

Strength training can also boost your confidence and self-esteem as you start seeing changes in your body. Studies in both men and women document the psychological benefits. For example, in a Montana State University study, 341 women ages 23 to 87 did a strength training class twice a week for about 10 weeks. As a result, they significantly improved their body image, became more active throughout the day, and reported enjoying physical activity more.

Here are some other ways in which strength training improves specific health conditions.

Slowing bone loss

Like muscle mass, bone strength starts to decline earlier than you might imagine, slipping at an average rate of 1% per year after age 40—and even more steeply for menopausal women, who can lose up to 20% of bone mass in five to seven years at that time of life. You can lose a fair amount of bone density and still remain in the normal range, but if bone loss occurs at a steeper rate, it can cause your bones to become weak and porous—a condition known as osteoporosis. About 10 million Americans have osteoporosis, and another 44 million are at risk for it.

Numerous studies have shown that weight-bearing exercise—defined as any exercise in which your body supports its own weight and works against gravity—can play a role in slowing bone loss. Several studies show it can even build a small amount of bone. Activities that put stress on bones stimulate extra deposits of calcium and nudge bone-forming cells into action. The tugging and pushing on bone that occur during strength and power training provide the stress. The result is stronger, denser bones.

Even weight-bearing aerobic exercise, like walking or running, can help your bones, but there are a couple of caveats. Generally, higher-impact activities have a more pronounced effect on bone than lower-impact aerobics. Velocity is also a factor; jogging or fast-paced aerobics will do more to strengthen bone than more leisurely movement. And keep in mind that only those bones that bear the load of the exercise will benefit. For example, walking or running protects only the bones in your lower body, including your hips.

By contrast, a well-rounded strength training program that works out all the major muscle groups can benefit practically all of your bones. Of particular interest, it targets bones of the hips, spine, and wrists, which, along with the ribs, are the sites most likely to fracture. Also, by enhancing strength and stability, resistance workouts reduce the likelihood of falls, which can lead to fractures.

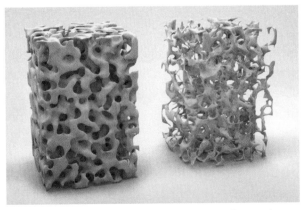

With age, both your muscles and your bones tend to weaken. Bones become more porous and less dense (like the example on the right, above) and are therefore more prone to fracture.

Improving insulin sensitivity

About 34 million people in the United States have diabetes, and 88 million people have prediabetes. If you have diabetes, strength training can help you better control your blood sugar levels—and if you don't have the condition, strength training can reduce your risk of developing type 2 diabetes (the most common form of the disease) by making the body more sensitive to insulin and improving blood sugar control.

Skeletal muscle serves as a reservoir for glucose, penning up sugar in the form of glycogen and doling it out as necessary to fuel your muscles' movement. The more muscle you have, the more efficiently your body can sop up circulating blood sugar.

While aerobic exercise provides more protection against diabetes than strength training does, the best protection comes when you do both types of exercise. According to a Harvard University analysis of more than 32,000 men in the Health Professionals Follow-up Study, men who did 150 minutes of cardio a week reduced their risk of developing type 2 diabetes by 52%. Those who did an equal amount of strength training cut their risk by 34%. But doing both cardio and strength training for a total of 150 minutes a week—so no extra time needed—reduced their risk by 59%. Similar research in women showed a 30% to 40% reduction.

And you get benefits after just one workout. Research shows that a single cardio or strength session speeds the rate at which glucose enters the muscles. Note that the effect dissipates in two to four days, however, unless the activity is repeated. Regular workouts also help the body remain sensitive to insulin rather than succumbing to the creeping insulin resistance that often develops as people get older.

When diabetes does develop, strength training can help control it. One study of older adults with type 2 diabetes found that four months of strength train-

Exercise can improve your insulin sensitivity and in the process, help control diabetes. Both aerobic exercise and strength training play a role.

ing improved blood sugar control so much that seven out of 10 volunteers were able to reduce their dosage of diabetes medicine. The evidence supporting strength training's effect on diabetes is so compelling that the American Diabetes Association recommends that anyone with diabetes should do at least two strength workouts a week.

Even when insulin is not being produced in normal amounts by the body—as is the case with type 1 diabetes—lowering blood sugar through strength training can reduce the amount of injected insulin a person needs to keep blood sugar under control.

Easing joint pain

Strong muscles support and protect your joints, easing pain and stiffness and reducing your risk of developing osteoarthritis. In this form of arthritis, which can show up in your 40s or 50s, the cartilage that cushions your joints gradually wears away and abnormal bony growths develop in the joint. But when strong muscles contract, they take pressure off the joints, reducing this kind of wear and tear. For instance, a study published in the journal *Arthritis and Rheumatology* suggested that greater quadriceps strength reduces cartilage loss in the knee. Without strong quadriceps, the joint bears the brunt of the impact from walking, running, or other weight-bearing activities.

Strength training may also enhance range of motion in many joints, so you'll be able to bend and reach with greater ease. In a randomized controlled study of 32 older men, after 16 weeks of workouts, men doing strength training alone or combined with cardiovascular training had significantly greater range of motion in all five of the joints tested than men who remained inactive. Among those doing just cardiovascular activities, range of motion improved in only one of the joints that were tested.

If you do develop osteoarthritis, strength training

can ease pain and improve quality of life. In one study, women in their 60s or 70s who had either knee osteo-arthritis or a knee replacement did strength training twice a week for 13 weeks. By the end of the study, the women had improved their ability to walk, climb stairs, and balance.

People with rheumatoid arthritis can also benefit, since muscle weakness is common among those with this illness. One study reported that moderate or high-intensity strength training was more effective at increasing or maintaining muscle strength than low-intensity programs. A key to reaping long-term benefits, though, was consistency with the training program.

Exercise is a natural mood booster. It can dispel bad moods, but even more remarkable, it can help alleviate clinical depression, especially when used in conjunction with therapy and medication.

Other conditions

There are many more conditions that may benefit from regular strength training. Here are a few. (Research on power training for these problems is still in its infancy.)

Depression. Strength training may help with mild to moderate depression by restoring lost abilities, which can boost confidence and open up new options for pleasurable activities; it may also alleviate dependence on others. One study of adults ages 60 and older with depression found that high-intensity strength training was more effective at reducing depressive symptoms than low-intensity strength training, so choose challenging weights and keep working out regularly. Combining exercise with therapy or with both therapy and medication may yield the best results.

Cancer. Despite improvements, most cancer treatments still have unpleasant side effects such as fatigue, physical discomfort, impaired sleep, and emotional distress, which can degrade quality of life. But exercise, including strength training, can help. In one study, women who had breast cancer started a program of either resistance training or cardio exercise during chemotherapy. Both groups saw improvements in their strength, endurance, and quality of life, but the weight lifters had slightly greater gains.

And for women suffering from lymphedema (arm swelling after breast cancer surgery), strength training may also offer some relief. A classic study published in *The New England Journal of Medicine* found that those who did weight training twice a week for 13 weeks reported fewer symptoms and flare-ups. More recently, a 2019 study showed that even when women trained with heavy weights, they were not at increased risk for lymphedema. The findings call into question the long-held medical view that women who have had breast cancer surgery should avoid stressing the arm for fear that muscle strain could worsen arm swelling.

Lyme disease. Annually, 300,000 Americans are diagnosed with Lyme disease, and over 40% of them have persistent symptoms such as pain, fatigue, and a poor quality of life. But it looks like just a little bit of strength training may have a big impact. Just one set of five exercises done three times a week for four weeks resulted in a sevenfold increase in the number of days people said that they felt healthy and full of energy, according to a small pilot study. More research is needed, but if you have Lyme disease, it might be worth investing in some dumbbells.

Fibromyalgia. This disorder, which is more common in women than men, is characterized by widespread musculoskeletal pain, increased sensitivity to pain, impaired physical abilities, fatigue, and distress. There is currently no cure for fibromyalgia, but exercise, including strength training, appears to offer some hope. A Swedish study of 130 women with fibromyalgia found that those who participated in strength training workouts twice a week for 15 weeks got stronger, reduced their pain by 23%, were better able to deal with their pain, and participated in everyday activities more than the women who didn't exercise. ♥

Should you check with your doctor first?

If you're already doing strength training, you've quite likely taken the necessary precautions. However, if you're new to this type of exercise—or if you're looking to crank up the intensity of your workouts by doing the Medicine Ball Workout (page 33) or Kettlebell Workout (page 37) or adding plyometrics (see "Bonus power moves: Plyometrics," page 42) to your routine—it's wise to consult with your doctor or physical therapist before starting. That's especially true if you have not been active recently, if you're a smoker or have quit within the past six months, or if you have any injuries or an unstable chronic health condition, including these:

- heart disease (or multiple risk factors for it)
- a respiratory ailment, such as asthma
- high blood pressure
- joint or bone disease
- a neurologic illness
- diabetes
- a joint replacement.

Some conditions, such as unstable angina or an abdominal aortic aneurysm (a weak spot in the wall of the body's main artery) can make strength or power training unsafe. Other problems—for example, a joint

If you have any injuries or an unstable chronic health condition, or if you're looking to crank up the intensity of your workout, you should consult your doctor first to make sure it's safe for you.

▶ Warning signs

Signs of an emergency. If you experience any of these symptoms during or after exercise, call 911 or see a doctor immediately:

- ✔ upper-body discomfort, including chest pain, aching, burning, tightness, or a feeling of uncomfortable fullness
- ✔ significant or persistent wheezing, shortness of breath, or dizziness that takes longer than five minutes to go away
- ✔ faintness or loss of consciousness.

These warning signs pertain to any kind of exercise—strength training and aerobic exercise alike.

Signs that should prompt a call for advice. Persistent or intense muscle pain that starts during a workout or right afterward, or muscle soreness that lasts more than one to two weeks, also merits a call to your doctor. (This is in contrast to normal muscle soreness, which starts 12 to 48 hours after a workout and gradually improves.) You should also call your doctor if the routine you've been doing for a while without discomfort starts to cause you pain.

injury or cataract treatment—may make it unsafe temporarily (see "When exercise is not advisable," page 14); in that case, wait until your doctor gives you the go-ahead. One helpful resource for gauging your ability is the Canadian Society for Exercise Physiologists' Get Active Questionnaire (GAQ). You can find it at www.health.harvard.edu/GAQ.

Generally speaking, anyone who is healthy or has a well-controlled health problem, such as high blood pressure or diabetes, can safely do the strength and power training workouts in this report, as long as they start with the Basic Workout (page 22) or Resistance Band Workout (page 27) and gradually progress to the more challenging workouts that follow. However, you should stop immediately if you experience certain distress signals from your body (see "Warning signs," above).

Questions for your doctor

When you ask your doctor whether you should observe any restrictions, it's important to explain exactly what sort of program you hope to undertake. Here are three good questions to ask:

- Do I have any health conditions that would be adversely affected by strength or power training or other types of exercise? (For example, people with poorly controlled high blood pressure generally should avoid isometric exercises, which can raise blood pressure considerably.)
- Will my medications affect exercise in any way or vice versa? (People taking insulin or medicine to lower blood sugar may need to adjust the dose when they exercise, for example.)
- Should I limit the types or intensity of exercises I do? (For example, people who have had a hip replacement may be told to avoid bringing their knees to their chest.)

If you are recovering from certain health problems, your doctor may give you a referral to a physiatrist—a medical doctor who specializes in physical medicine and rehabilitation—or a physical therapist. While physiatrists may tell you what exercises and movements not to do, they generally leave it up to physical therapists to design exercise programs for their patients. Insurance coverage for these services varies, so check with your insurance provider to learn more.

Your heart rate naturally increases during exercise. You should also be aware that during weight lifting, holding your breath can raise your blood pressure. Try counting out loud to make yourself breathe.

When exercise is not advisable

The National Institute on Aging notes that there are also specific reasons to hold off temporarily on exercise until a doctor advises you that it's safe to resume. These are not specific to strength training; you should not do aerobic exercise, either, if you have any of the following:

- a hernia
- sores on feet or ankles that aren't healing
- hot, swollen joints
- difficulty walking, or lasting pain, after a fall
- blood clots
- a detached or bleeding retina, cataract surgery or a lens implant, or laser eye surgery
- chest pains
- fever (it is usually safe to start exercising again at lighter intensity once the fever has subsided and you feel better)
- irregular, fast, or fluttery heartbeat.

Tips for people with specific conditions

If you have heart disease, diabetes, arthritis, or osteoporosis, it is imperative that you speak with your doctor before you start strength or power training. Once he or she has signed off on your exercise plans, here are some tips that may help you get more out of your workouts and avoid injury.

If you have heart disease

- Be sure to breathe while lifting and lowering weights. Holding your breath while straining can raise blood pressure dangerously. Counting out loud as you exhale may help.
- Be aware that many drugs given to help treat heart disease may affect you when you're exercising. Beta blockers, for example, keep heart rate artificially low; that means your pulse is not a good indicator of how vigorously you are exercising. Vasodilators and ACE inhibitors may make you more prone to dizziness from a drop in blood pressure if your post-exercise cool-down is too short. Talk with your doctor about the medications you take. If you work with an exercise professional, be sure he or she understands the potential effects, too.

If you have diabetes

- Talk with your doctor about adjusting your medications before starting or increasing a strength training program. Exercise, including strength training, uses glucose, so it may affect the dose of medication you need and maybe even the timing of your doses.
- Keep glucose tablets with you when you exercise in case your blood sugar drops precipitously, a condition called hypoglycemia. Signs of hypoglycemia include sweating, trembling, dizziness, hunger, and confusion.
- Wear a diabetes bracelet or ID tag and carry phone numbers of your emergency contacts in case of emergency while exercising.

If you have arthritis

- Schedule workouts for times of the day when your medications are working well, in order to reduce inflammation and pain. For example, avoid morning workouts if stiffness is at its worst then.
- Before exercise, apply heat to sore joints or take a warm shower or bath. After exercise, cold packs may be helpful.
- If you have rheumatoid arthritis or another form of inflammatory arthritis, include some gentle stretching after you warm up. Inflammation weakens the tendons that tie muscle to bone, making them more susceptible to injury. Remember to use slow movements during your warm-up, and gradually extend your range of motion.
- If you have rheumatoid arthritis, add more rest time to your routine when your condition flares up to reduce inflammation, pain, and fatigue. When it calms down, you can exercise more. Staying active with frequent rest breaks tends to help more than long periods spent in bed.
- Exercise within a comfortable range of motion. If an entire exercise causes significant pain, stop

If you have arthritis, it's a good idea to apply heat to sore joints before exercising, in order to reduce pain and stiffness. A warm shower or bath will also work.

doing it! Discuss other options with your trainer or physical therapist.
- Generally, you should avoid doing strength or power training with actively inflamed joints, at least until the inflammation eases. In some cases, water workouts may be a better choice than strength or power training.

If you have osteoporosis

- Protect your spine. Avoid activities and exercises that require you to bend your spine, especially while lifting a weight.
- Bend your knees when picking up weights to do exercises. You might want to store your weights on a shelf so they are easy to access without injuring your spine.
- Consider trying exercises, such as stair climbing, squats, or lunges, using a weighted vest, especially if you are a postmenopausal woman (see "Try a weighted vest," page 49). Some studies have shown that progressive training using a weighted vest can increase the development of new bone in the hip and pelvis and improve balance. ◗

Getting started

Where should strength and power training fit into your exercise plans? What equipment, if any, will you need? This chapter answers those questions and explains the basic terminology used in our strength and power workouts. You will also learn what else a well-rounded exercise program should include in addition to strength and power training.

A few pieces of basic equipment are all you need to work out at home. All of these items—weights, resistance bands, kettlebells, and more—can be purchased online or at sporting goods stores.

Buying equipment

The equipment you need for strength and power training depends on the workouts you choose. In this report, there are four different workouts that require different kinds of equipment—dumbbells, resistance bands, a medicine ball, or kettlebells. We recommend that you start with either the Basic Workout (with dumbbells) or the Resistance Band Workout. Once you've mastered one or both of these, you can move on to one of the other workouts.

Below you'll find descriptions of what you need for each workout. You can buy all of this equipment online. You may also be able to find it at department, discount, or sporting goods stores.

For all the workouts, you should also have a non-slip exercise mat. (A thick carpet will do in a pinch.) The plyometrics exercises require nothing but a good pair of shoes with sturdy support.

For the Basic Workout
- Dumbbells in a few different weights. Depending on your current strength, you might start with as little as a set of 2-pound and 5-pound weights or 5-pound and 8-pound weights. Add heavier weights as needed. Prices start around $10 for a set and increase for heavier weights. Alternatively, you can buy adjustable dumbbells that offer a variety of weight ranges—for example, from 2.5 to 12.5 pounds or from 5 to 25 pounds. Prices start at about $70 for a set.
- A sturdy chair, preferably without armrests.

For the Resistance Band Workout
- Resistance bands or tubes in a variety of resistance levels, designated by color. Bands look like big, wide rubber bands, while the tubes are narrow, have handles, and tend to be more durable. Bands and tubes provide more resistance on the eccentric contraction than dumbbells. Prices start at about $10, and many are sold in sets so you get a variety of resistance levels.
- Heavy furniture, poles, or railings to anchor the band for certain moves. In a pinch, you could have someone else hold the band for you. Just make sure that he or she is stronger than you are.

For the Medicine Ball Workout
- Medicine balls, which are about the size of a soccer ball and come in a variety of weights. You can lift or toss them to work your muscles in new ways. Start with a lightweight ball, about 4 to 8 pounds. Some medicine balls bounce, while others don't. You can use either type for the routine in this report. Prices start around $20.

For the Kettlebell Workout
- Kettlebells, which look like a ball or bell with a handle. Unlike dumbbells, which you grip at the center of the mass, you grip kettlebells outside of their center of mass. This requires you to exert

more muscle force to control the weight, providing a more challenging workout. The lightest kettlebell is usually 5 pounds. Prices start at about $25. Most are sold individually, but some sets are available. There are also adjustable types so you can get multiple weights in one kettlebell.

Frequently asked questions

The answers to the following questions provide crucial information about strength and power training to ensure that you get a safe and effective workout.

How often should I do strength training?

According to the most recent Physical Activity Guidelines for Americans, issued by the U.S. Department of Health and Human Services, adults ages 18 to 64 should perform a complete strength training routine, about 20 to 30 minutes, two or three times a week. (Of course, once a week is better than not at all, if that's the most you can manage.) Allow at least 48 hours between sessions to let your muscles recover. So, if you do a strength workout on Monday, wait until at least Wednesday to do another one.

The fastest gains in strength are made in the first four to eight weeks; after that, expect progress to slow somewhat.

How often should I do power training?

The Physical Activity Guidelines for Americans do not address power training, but the American College of Sports Medicine (ACSM) has been advocating it for more than 10 years. Based on research, the ACSM recommends doing power training two or three times a week along with strength training. You can easily do that with the workouts in this report.

Do I still need to do aerobic workouts?

Yes! Aerobic activity is good for better heart health, lower blood pressure, improved diabetes management, sounder sleep, better immune function, sharper mental function, and more. See "Rounding out your exercise program," below, for guidelines on how often to do aerobic exercise.

Rounding out your exercise program

Strength training is only one piece of the exercise puzzle. According to experts, a well-rounded program should also include aerobic activity and flexibility exercises, and for older adults, balance exercises. Here's a summary of what you need. If all of this seems like more than you can manage, just start where you can and work up. The guidelines emphasize that any exercise is better than none, and even routine activity will help. The goal, they say, should be to move more and sit less.

Aerobic activity. Aerobic activity (also called cardiovascular exercise, or simply cardio) is exercise that speeds heart rate and breathing for sustained periods. Examples include walking, running, cycling, or swimming. According to the Physical Activity Guidelines for Americans from the U.S. Department of Health and Human Services, most adults should aim for at least 150 minutes of moderate aerobic activity a week, spread throughout the week.

If you kick up the intensity level of your workouts from moderate to vigorous intensity (say, from brisk walking to running), you can reduce your total amount of aerobic exercise from 150 minutes to 75 minutes a week—or plan an equivalent mix of the two for the appropriate amount of time. (Ten minutes of vigorous activity equals roughly 20 minutes of moderate activity.) There are various ways to determine how hard you are exercising. But this one, known informally as the "talk test," is simple and intuitive: if you can sing and do the activity, it is low intensity; if you can talk but not sing, it is moderate intensity; and if you can't sing or talk, it is vigorous or high intensity.

The guidelines note that if you can double the amount of aerobic exercise you do, you'll get even more health benefits.

Flexibility exercises. Stretches may expand your range of motion, keep muscles more limber, improve posture and balance, and help prevent falls. Warm muscles are less likely to be injured than cold muscles, so it's best to perform stretches as part of your cool-down following a workout. Or, if you prefer, you can stretch after a five- to 10-minute warm-up, during which you might walk or dance to some of your favorite songs. Consider activities such as yoga or tai chi, which help with balance as well as improving flexibility.

Balance exercises. Single-leg exercises and exercises that strengthen your back, abdomen, buttocks, and legs—like those in this report—will help improve balance, which in turn can help you avoid falls. Three sessions a week are recommended for older adults, who are most at risk of falling.

Training tips

The following guidelines apply to any strength training program you choose.

- Drink water throughout the day and whenever you exercise in order to prevent headaches and fatigue.

- Never sacrifice proper form and good posture for the sake of lifting heavier weights or going faster. It's easiest to learn good form through a class or one-on-one sessions with a well-trained exercise professional. If that's not possible, exercise in front of a mirror so you can check your form (see "Posture and alignment: Striking the right pose," page 19).

- Breathe out as you lift or exert force; breathe in as you lower or release. Don't hold your breath, as this can cause your blood pressure to rise. Counting out loud as you lift will prevent you from holding your breath.

- Focus on the muscles you are working. In a study from Denmark, participants increased muscle activity up to 35% when they thought about the muscles they were working as they performed the exercise. The more muscle activity, the better results you'll get.

- Isolate muscles by trying to move only the muscles you're exercising. This will prevent other muscles from helping out, thereby minimizing the strengthening benefits to the muscles you're trying to work. Don't rock or sway.

- Lift or push and release weights smoothly, without jerking. Jerky movements can sometimes lead to spraining or straining a muscle, tendon, or ligament.

- Don't lock your joints; always leave a slight bend in your knees and elbows when straightening out your legs and arms. Hyperextended joints can strain ligaments around the joint. This is especially important when doing jumping exercises like those in "Bonus power moves: Plyometrics," page 42.

- When moving your arms or legs, stick with a range that feels comfortable. These exercises should not cause pain while you are doing them. Over time, gradually extend your range of motion through exercise and stretching.

- Listen to your body, and cut back if you aren't able to finish a series of exercises or an exercise session, can't talk while exercising, feel faint after a session, feel tired during the day, or suffer joint aches and pains after a session.

- Build up slowly over time. Don't be so eager to see results that you risk hurting yourself by exercising too long or too often or by choosing too much weight. Remember that it's important to rest muscles for at least 48 hours between sessions.

- If you injure yourself, remember RICE (rest, ice, compression, and elevation). Rest the injured muscle. Ice it for 20 to 30 minutes every two to three hours during the first two or three days. Apply compression with an elastic bandage whenever you're out of bed until the swelling resolves. Elevate the injured area while resting or icing. Call your doctor for advice and information about managing pain or swelling. Wait until the injury heals before doing strength training on that muscle again, and start with a lower weight.

How much weight or resistance should I use?

Once you understand exactly how to do each exercise, choose a weight (or resistance level for bands) that allows you to do only the recommended number of repetitions (reps). The last one or two reps should be difficult. If you can't lift the weight at least the minimum number of reps, use a lighter weight or resistance (see "Training tips," above).

If you exercise regularly, your muscles will gradually adapt to the weight you are using so you can do more reps. When you can comfortably perform the maximum number of reps without completely tiring the muscle, it's time to increase the amount of weight.

How quickly (or slowly) should I lift the weights?

The speed, or tempo, at which you perform the exercises will vary depending on the type of exercise you are doing. Strength training exercises should be done at a 3–1–3 tempo. That means three seconds to lift the weight, one second to hold it in that position, and three seconds to lower the weight. For power training, you'll pick up the pace. You will do the lifting as quickly as possible while maintaining good form. The rest of the exercise is performed at the slower tempo used for strength training: You hold at the top of the move for one second, then take three seconds to lower. (See "Tempo," page 21, for more directions.)

How many sets of each exercise should I do?

Strength training aims to tire the muscles that are being worked. According to numerous scientific reviews, the best way to do this is to perform three sets of each exercise. (A set consists of a recommended number of reps.) That doesn't mean you should skip a workout if you have time for only one set—you get the most strength and toning benefits from the first set, especially if you're a beginner, with subsequent sets providing diminishing returns. However, the more you train, the more important it will be to do three sets in order to achieve the best results and continue gaining strength.

How long should I rest between sets?

Resting for one to three minutes between sets nets the best strength gains. The higher the intensity of your workout (meaning the heavier the weights you're lifting), the more rest you'll need. For most people, a minute or two is ample. During this time, your body generates hormonal and metabolic responses that build and strengthen muscles. In addition, resting enables your muscles to perform better on your next set. If you don't rest at all, your muscles may be too tired for you to lift with good form, increasing your risk of injury. Conversely, resting too long may also be risky, because your muscles cool down, making them more susceptible to injury.

If you don't want to wait one to three minutes, cutting rest time between sets to 30 seconds keeps your heart rate and calorie burn up, so you reap some aerobic and weight-loss benefits during a strength training session. It's wise to note, however, that this lessens strength and muscle gains. It's a trade-off that each person should evaluate. If you do choose to cut your rest time, adjust the amount of weight you are lifting to be sure you don't sacrifice good form.

Posture and alignment: Striking the right pose

Exercise is important, but if you don't do it right, you run the risk of injuring yourself. You will also slow gains because you aren't isolating muscles properly.

Posture helps more than you might think. In fact, good posture and alignment help anytime you're moving. For example, if you bend at your waist while doing arm curls or the overhead press (see page 25 for both exercises), this puts stress on your lower back that may result in an injury. And changing the posture or alignment of an exercise can change the muscles that are being worked.

For example, if you keep your elbows in close to your body during a push-up, you will work your triceps (the backs of your arms) more than your chest muscles. Depending upon the routine you are doing, that may be fine. For our routine, the kneeling push-up should target your chest muscles more, so the description tells you to point your elbows out to the sides. That's why it's important to read and follow the instructions carefully.

The exercises in our workouts often call for you to stand up straight. That means

- your chin is parallel to the floor
- both shoulders are back and down
- both wrists are firm and straight, not flexed upward or downward
- both hips are even
- both knees are pointed straight ahead
- both feet are pointed straight ahead
- body weight is distributed evenly on both feet.

In addition, it's important to maintain a neutral spine. A neutral spine takes into account the slight natural curves of the spine, but it's not flexed or arched. One way to find the neutral position is to lift your tailbone as far as comfortable to arch your lower back, then tuck your tailbone under to flatten your lower back. The spot approximately in the middle should be neutral. If you're not used to standing or sitting up straight, it may take a while for this to feel natural. When you are instructed to bend, do so at the hips, not at the waist, and keep your spine neutral and your core muscles contracted to protect your back.

Few of us have perfect posture, which is why it's so important to check your posture before and during each exercise. Each exercise in our workouts offers tips on good technique, so make sure you review them before trying the move. Looking in a mirror as you do exercises helps enormously. It enables you to observe your body position and correct sloppy form.

Paying attention as you perform upper-body exercises may also alert you to muscle imbalances based on whether your right or left side is dominant. If you notice this, focus on your weaker side to make sure it's not slacking off. Over time, this will help to even out the imbalance and give you a better workout. ♥

The workouts

This report includes four strength and power workouts that use different types of equipment—dumbbells, resistance bands, a medicine ball, and a kettlebell. In addition, there are plyometrics (jumping exercises) that you can add to any of the workouts once you've progressed through the other routines.

If you are new to strength training or have not been doing it regularly for the past month, we recommend that you start with the strength version of either the Basic Workout (page 22) or the Resistance Band Workout (page 27). For at least two to four weeks, follow the "strength" instructions for reps and tempo. These routines will help you build a strong foundation.

When you feel comfortable with these, you can turn either of the routines into a power workout by following the "power" instructions for reps and tempo. After another two to four weeks, you can advance to one of the other two workouts—the Medicine Ball Workout (page 33) or the Kettlebell Workout (page 37)—which incorporate both strength and power training. Give yourself another two to four weeks, and then you can add some high-impact, power-boosting plyometrics (page 42) to your routine, if you desire.

Don't forget to warm up before you begin, and cool down afterward. Then, spend a few minutes doing the stretching exercises to complete your workout.

Always remember to maintain good posture and alignment and follow our training tips to minimize your risk of injury.

Warm-up

Before doing any of the workouts, spend five to 10 minutes warming up all major muscle groups. A warm-up enables your body to ease into exercise. Your heart rate and breathing gradually increase, pumping more nutrient-rich, oxygenated blood to your muscles for exercise. Your joints become more lubricated and your muscles more pliable so they perform better, and you're less susceptible to discomfort or even an injury.

Excellent ways to warm up include marching in place and gently swinging your arms, walking on a treadmill, pedaling an exercise bike, or mimicking the workout exercises without holding any weights. Start slowly, and gradually increase your pace.

Note that stretching is no longer recommended as a warm-up. Classic "static" stretches—where you move into a position that stretches a certain muscle group and hold that position—may increase your risk of injury if your muscles are cold, so it's best to save these stretches for during or after a workout. By contrast, "dynamic" stretching involves a movement pattern intended to take specific muscles through a full range of motion and can serve as a warm-up; to see a short routine, go to www.health.harvard.edu/dynamic-stretches.

A good warm-up gradually increases your breathing and heart rate, helping to ease your body into exercise. Five to 10 minutes of walking or marching in place will do the trick.

© Anchiy | Getty Images

Cool-down

Cooling down slows breathing and heartbeat, gradually routing blood back into its normal circulatory patterns. This helps prevent a sudden drop in blood pressure that can cause dizziness, especially if you bend over or straighten up quickly (a reaction called postural hypotension). After your workout, spend five to 10 minutes cooling down by walking around. The more intense your workout and the higher your heart rate, the longer your cool-down should be. Don't forget to stretch afterward (see "Stretches," page 46).

Key to the instructions

Each of the exercises in our workouts includes certain directions—including your starting position and the movement you will make during each exercise—along with tips and techniques to help. We also use certain terms you'll need to know.

Repetitions (reps). Each time you perform the movement in an exercise, that's called a rep. If you cannot do all the reps at first, just do what you can, and then gradually increase reps as you improve. When you are training for strength, aim for eight to 12 reps. For power training, you'll do fewer reps—six to 10—but at a faster pace (see "Tempo," below).

Set. One set is a specific number of repetitions. For example, eight to 12 reps often make a single set. Usually, we suggest doing one to three sets.

Tempo. This tells you the count for the key movements in an exercise. For example, 3–1–3 means lift a weight in three counts, hold for one count, then lower it on a count of three. Exercises with more parts have more numbers, and some, like the halo (page 38), have

Stretching helps loosen tight muscles and keeps you limber. A good time to stretch is after exercising, because your muscles are most pliable then. Include it in your cool-down session.

only one number, meaning the exercise is one fluid movement.

Hold. While most exercises have a hold as part of the tempo, the stretching exercises list "Hold" as a separate line, since that is the focus of stretches. It tells you the number of seconds to hold each stretch.

Rest. Resting between sets gives your muscles a chance to recharge and helps you maintain good form. Except for the warm-up and cool-down activities, we specify a range of time to rest. How much of this time you need will differ depending on your level of fitness and how heavy your weights are (see "How long should I rest between sets?" on page 19).

In addition, each set of instructions offers options to "make it easier" or "make it harder." These variations modify the exercise to be less challenging (for beginners or those with health concerns) or to increase the difficulty (for more advanced exercisers). ◗

Basic Workout

The Basic Workout is good for everyone. If you're new to strength training—or haven't been exercising for a month or more—this dumbbell and bodyweight routine is a great starting point. But even if you lift weights regularly, this workout can help by targeting muscles in new ways. As you grow stronger, you can continue to challenge yourself with this routine by using heavier weights, by doing the "make it harder" variations for each exercise, or by turning the strength workout into a power routine.

To convert the strength routine into a power workout: Simply change the tempos of the exercises, as indicated in the instructions for each exercise. Each one includes two different tempos—the slower one for strength and the faster one for power. For example, in the bent-over row, instead of lifting to a count of 3, holding for 1, and lowering for another 3, you would lift to a count of just 1, then hold for 1, and lower for 3.

(To see an example illustrating the difference, go to the video at www.health.harvard.edu/strength-to-power.)

If you're a beginner: Follow the instructions for the standard, strength form of each exercise for at least two weeks before moving on to the power variations or the "make it harder" options. That way, you will become familiar with the exercises and build a base of strength to avoid injury as you progress.

You should do at least two weeks of power training before moving on to the more advanced Medicine Ball Workout or Kettlebell Workout. These two workouts incorporate both strength and power training.

For variety, you can alternate the Basic Workout with the Resistance Band Workout, which is another good routine for beginners.

The editors would like to thank Philip L. Penny and Michele Stanten for serving as models for the workouts.

---

1 Reverse lunge

Easier

Muscles worked: Gluteus, quadriceps, hamstrings, gastrocnemius

Reps: 8–12 for strength, 6–10 for power
Sets: 1–3
Tempo: 3–1–3 for strength, 3–1–1 for power
Rest: 30–90 seconds between sets

Starting position: Stand up straight with your feet together and your arms at your sides, holding dumbbells.

Movement: Step back onto the ball of your left foot, bend your knees, and lower into a lunge. Your right knee should align over your right ankle, and your left knee should point toward (but not touch) the floor. Push off your back (left) foot to stand up and return to the starting position. Repeat, stepping back with your right foot to do the lunge on the opposite side. This is one rep.

Tips and techniques:
- Keep your spine neutral when lowering into the lunge.
- Don't lean forward or back.
- As you bend your knees, lower the back knee directly down to the floor with the thigh perpendicular to the floor.

Make it easier: Do stationary lunges, so that you're not stepping back with one foot at the beginning of each lunge. Simply stand with one foot in front of the other and bend your knees. Finish all reps, then switch legs and repeat to complete one set. Or, do lunges without weights.

Make it harder: Step forward into the lunges, or use heavier weights.

② Kneeling push-up

Muscles worked: Pectoralis, deltoids, triceps, rectus abdominis, erector spinae, gluteus

Reps: 8–12 for strength, 6–10 for power
Sets: 1–3
Tempo: 3–1–3 for strength, 3–1–1 for power
Rest: 30–90 seconds between sets

Starting position: Begin on the floor on all fours with your hands slightly more than shoulder-width apart. Walk your hands forward and lower your hips so your body is at a 45° angle to the floor and forms a straight line from head to knees.

Movement: Bend your elbows out to the sides and slowly lower your upper body toward the floor until your elbows are bent about 90°. Press against the floor and straighten your arms to return to the starting position.

Tips and techniques:
• Keep your head in line with your spine.
• Keep your core muscles tight to prevent your back from arching too much.

Make it easier: Stand up and do push-ups with your hands against a wall or a countertop.

Make it harder: Lift your knees off the floor and do push-ups supporting yourself on your hands and the toes and balls of your feet.

Harder

③ Wood chop

Muscles worked: Pectoralis, deltoids, gluteus, obliques, quadriceps, hamstrings, rectus abdominis, erector spinae

Reps: 8–12 on each side for strength, 6–10 on each side for power
Sets: 1–3
Tempo: 3–1–3 for strength, 1–1–3 for power
Rest: 30–90 seconds between sets

Starting position: Stand with your feet about shoulder-width apart and hold a dumbbell with both hands. Hinge forward at your hips and bend your knees to sit back into a slight squat. Rotate your torso to the right and extend your arms to hold the dumbbell on the outside of your right knee.

Movement: Straighten your legs to stand up as you rotate your torso to the left and raise the weight diagonally across your body and up to the left, above your shoulder, while keeping your arms extended. In a chopping motion, slowly bring the dumbbell down and across your body toward the outside of your right knee. This is one rep. Finish all reps, then repeat on the other side. This completes one set.

Tips and techniques:
• Keep your spine neutral and your shoulders down and back.
• Reach only as far as is comfortable.
• Keep your knees no farther forward than your toes when you squat.

Make it easier: Do the exercise without a dumbbell.

Make it harder: Use a heavier dumbbell.

4 Bent-over row

Muscles worked: Latissimus dorsi, trapezius, rhomboids, deltoids, biceps

Reps: 8–12 with each arm for strength, 6–10 with each arm for power
Sets: 1–3
Tempo: 3–1–3 for strength, 1–1–3 for power
Rest: 30–90 seconds between sets

Starting position: Stand with a weight in your left hand and a bench or sturdy chair at your right side. Place your right hand and knee on the bench or chair seat. Let your left arm hang directly under your left shoulder, fully extended toward the floor. Your spine should be neutral and your shoulders and hips squared.

Movement: Squeeze your shoulder blades together, then bend your elbow to slowly lift the weight toward your ribs. Return to the starting position. Finish all reps, then repeat with the opposite arm. This completes one set.

Tips and techniques:
- Keep your shoulders squared throughout.
- Keep your elbow close to your side as you lift the weight.
- Keep your head in line with your spine.

Make it easier: Use a lighter weight.

Make it harder: Use a heavier weight.

5 Bridge

Muscles worked: Gluteus, hamstrings, erector spinae

Reps: 8–12 for strength, 6–10 for power
Sets: 1–3
Tempo: 3–1–3 for strength, 1–1–3 for power
Rest: 30–90 seconds between sets

Starting position: Lie on your back with your knees bent and feet flat on the floor, hip-width apart and parallel to each other. Place your arms at your sides, palms up. Relax your shoulders against the floor.

Movement: Tighten your buttocks, then lift your hips up off the floor as high as is comfortable. Keep your hips even and spine neutral. Return to the starting position.

Tips and techniques:
- Don't press your hands or arms against the floor to help you lift.
- Keep your shoulders, hips, knees, and feet evenly aligned.
- Keep your shoulders down and relaxed against the floor.

Make it easier: Lift your buttocks just slightly off the floor.

Make it harder: Extend one leg off the floor to do one-leg bridges.

Harder

QUICK BASIC WORKOUT

On days when you feel that you just don't have time for a full workout, do this abbreviated routine. Some exercise is better than none!

- Kneeling push-up (page 23)
- Wood chop (page 23)
- Bent-over row (above)
- Superman (page 25)

6 Superman

Muscles worked: Deltoids, latissimus dorsi, erector spinae, gluteus, hamstrings

Reps: 8–12 for strength, 6–10 for power
Sets: 1–3
Tempo: 3–1–3 for strength, 1–1–3 for power
Rest: 30–90 seconds between sets

Starting position: Lie facedown on the floor with your arms extended, palms down, and your legs extended.

Movement: Simultaneously lift your arms, head, chest, and legs up off the floor as high as is comfortable. Hold. Return to the starting position.

Tips and techniques:
• Tighten your buttocks before lifting.
• Don't look up.
• Keep your shoulders down, away from your ears.

Make it easier: Lift your right arm and left leg while keeping the opposite arm and leg on the floor. Switch sides with each rep.

Make it harder: Hold in the "up" position for three to five seconds before lowering.

7 Overhead press

Muscles worked: Deltoids, triceps

Reps: 8–12 for strength, 6–10 for power
Sets: 1–3
Tempo: 3–1–3 for strength, 1–1–3 for power
Rest: 30–90 seconds between sets

Starting position: Stand tall with your feet about shoulder-width apart, your chest lifted, and shoulders back and down. Hold a dumbbell in each hand at shoulder height with your palms facing forward and elbows pointing out to the sides.

Movement: Slowly raise the weights straight up until your arms are fully extended. Hold. Slowly lower the dumbbells back to the starting position.

Tips and techniques:
• Keep your abs tight.
• Keep your spine neutral and your shoulders down and back.
• Don't pull your elbows back in starting position.

Make it easier: Sit on a chair, or use lighter weights.

Make it harder: Use heavier weights.

8 Arm curl

Muscles worked: Biceps

Reps: 8–12 for strength, 6–10 for power
Sets: 1–3
Tempo: 3–1–3 for strength, 1–1–3 for power
Rest: 30–90 seconds between sets

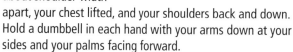

Starting position: Stand tall with your feet about shoulder-width apart, your chest lifted, and your shoulders back and down. Hold a dumbbell in each hand with your arms down at your sides and your palms facing forward.

Movement: Slowly bend your elbows, lifting the dumbbells toward your shoulders. Hold. Slowly lower the dumbbells, straightening your arms back to the starting position.

Tips and techniques:
• Keep your abs tight.
• Keep your spine neutral and your shoulders down and back.
• Keep your upper arms still and your elbows close to your sides.

Make it easier: Sit in a chair, or use lighter weights.

Make it harder: Use heavier weights.

9 Side plank

Muscles worked: Erector spinae, rectus abdominis, obliques, transverse abdominis

Reps: 2–4 on each side for strength, 6–10 on each side for power
Sets: 1 for strength, 1–3 for power
Tempo: Hold the plank position 15–60 seconds for strength; use tempo of 1–1–3 for power
Rest: 30–90 seconds between reps (for strength) or sets (for power)

Starting position: Lie in a straight line on your right side. Support your upper body on your right forearm with your shoulder aligned directly over your elbow. Stack your left foot on top of your right foot. Rest your left hand on your side.

Movement: Tighten your abdominal muscles. Exhale as you lift your right hip and right leg off the floor and raise your left arm toward the ceiling. Keeping shoulders and hips in a straight line, balance on your right forearm and the side of your right foot. Hold. Return to the starting position. This is one rep. Fin-

ish all reps, then repeat on your left side. This completes one set.

Tips and techniques:

- Keep your head and spine neutral, and align your shoulder over your elbow.
- Focus on lifting the bottom hip.
- Keep your shoulders down and back.

Make it easier: Bend at your knees and put your feet behind you. Keep your knees and lower legs on the floor as you lift your hips. Keep your hand on your hip.

Make it harder: Lift your top foot up as you hold.

Easier

Harder

10 Reverse fly

Muscles worked: Deltoids, rhomboids, trapezius

Reps: 8–12 for strength, 6–10 for power
Sets: 1–3
Tempo: 3–1–3 for strength, 1–1–3 for power
Rest: 30–90 seconds between sets

Starting position: Sit on the edge of a chair, holding a weight in each hand. Hinge forward at your hips, bringing your chest toward your thighs and keeping your back in a straight line. Your arms should hang next to your calves with your palms facing toward your body and thumbs pointing forward.

Movement: Squeeze your shoulder blades together, then slowly lift the weights out to the sides until your arms are at about shoulder height. Keep your elbows soft, not locked. Pause, then return to the starting position.

Tips and techniques:

- Throughout the movement, squeeze your shoulder blades together.

- Control the movement without using any momentum.
- Exhale as you lift.

Make it easier: Use lighter weights or no weights.

Make it harder: Use heavier weights. ▼

YOU'RE NOT DONE YET

See "Stretches," page 46, for a set of eight stretches to end your routine. Stretching helps to prevent stiffness and preserve flexibility and range of motion.

Resistance Band Workout

Here is another routine that's good for all levels. And since resistance bands are lightweight and packable, they are a great option for anyone who travels a lot. That means there's no excuse for missing a strength workout when you're on the road. Bands also target some muscles such as the latissimus dorsi that are harder to work with dumbbells. In addition, they place more consistent tension on the muscles throughout the range of motion. With dumbbells, the tension varies. Both are beneficial, which is why it's good to mix up your routine.

If you're a beginner: Follow the instructions for the standard form of each exercise for at least two weeks before moving on to the power versions or the "make it harder" variations. This will allow you to become familiar with the exercises and build a base of strength to avoid injury as you progress.

If you have experience in strength training: You can use bands that offer greater resistance. If that's not hard enough, you can hold dumbbells (start with light weights) as you do the band exercises to get a really challenging workout that offers the best of both types of equipment.

Everyone should do at least two weeks of power training (beginners may want to do more) before moving on to the more advanced Medicine Ball Workout and Kettlebell Workout, which incorporate both strength and power training. Feel free to alternate the Resistance Band Workout with the Basic Workout for variety.

1 Upright row

Muscles worked: Deltoids, trapezius, biceps

Reps: 8–12 for strength, 6–10 for power
Sets: 1–3
Tempo: 3–1–3 for strength, 1–1–3 for power
Rest: 30–90 seconds between sets

Starting position: Place the band under both feet. Grasp each end of the band, so the ends of the band hang inside your hands toward each other. Stand tall with your arms extending down in front of you.

Movement: Bend your elbows out to the sides and pull the band to chest height. Hold. Slowly extend your arms and return to the starting position, resisting the pull of the band.

Tips and techniques:
• Don't arch your back, and keep your abs tight.
• Keep your shoulders down and back, away from your ears.
• Keep your wrists straight, in line with your arms.

Easier

Make it easier: Stand on the band with only one foot so there is more slack in the band. Alternatively, you can place your hands closer to the ends of the band for less resistance, or use a lighter resistance band.

Make it harder: Place your hands closer to the center of the band for more resistance, or use a heavier resistance band.

2 Chest press

Muscles worked: Pectoralis, deltoids, triceps

Reps: 8–12 for strength, 6–10 for power
Sets: 1–3
Tempo: 3–1–3 for strength, 1–1–3 for power
Rest: 30–90 seconds between sets

Starting position: Stand tall with your feet about shoulder-width apart. Place a band across your upper back and under your arms. Hold each end with your arms bent, elbows pointing out and your hands by your armpits, palms down.

Movement: Extend your arms straight out in front of you at chest height, stretching the band. Slowly bend your arms and return to the starting position, resisting the pull of the band.

Tips and techniques:
• Don't arch your back, and keep your abs tight.
• Keep your shoulders down and back, away from your ears.
• Keep your wrists straight, in line with your arms.

Make it easier: Place your hands closer to the ends of the band for less resistance, or use a lighter resistance band. You can also do this move lying faceup on the floor with your legs bent.

Make it harder: Place your hands closer to the center of the band for more resistance, or use a heavier resistance band.

Easier

3 Pull-down

Muscles worked: Latissimus dorsi, biceps

Reps: 8–12 for strength, 6–10 for power
Sets: 1–3
Tempo: 3–1–3 for strength, 1–1–3 for power
Rest: 30–90 seconds between sets

Starting position: Stand tall with your feet about shoulder-width apart. Hold a band overhead with your arms extended and your hands about 12 to 18 inches apart.

Movement: Bend your elbows slightly and pull your hands down, stretching the band, to about shoulder level. Slowly raise your arms back overhead to the starting position, resisting the pull of the band.

Tips and techniques:
• Don't arch your back, and keep your abs tight.
• Keep your shoulders down and back, away from your ears.
• Keep your wrists straight, in line with your arms.

Make it easier: Place your hands closer to the ends of the band for less resistance, or use a lighter resistance band.

Make it harder: Place your hands closer to the center of the band for more resistance, or use a heavier resistance band.

4 Seated row with rotation

Muscles worked: Rhomboids, latissimus dorsi, biceps, obliques

Reps: 8–12 for strength, 6–10 for power
Sets: 1–3
Tempo: 3–1–3 for strength, 1–1–3 for power
Rest: 30–90 seconds between sets

Starting position: Sit on the floor with your legs bent slightly and the band wrapped around the arches of your feet. Grasp each end of the band with your arms extended, palms facing each other.

Movement: Bend your left elbow and pull the band toward your rib cage, keeping your left elbow close to your body and pointing behind you. As you pull, rotate your torso to the left. Hold. Slowly extend your arm and return to the starting position, resisting the pull of the band. Repeat with your right arm. This is one rep.

Tips and techniques:
• Don't lean back as you pull the band.
• Keep your shoulders down and back, away from your ears.
• Keep your wrists straight, in line with your arms.

Make it easier: Place your hands closer to the ends of the band for less resistance, or use a lighter resistance band. You can also do the seated row without the rotation.

Make it harder: Place your hands closer to the center of the band for more resistance, or use a heavier resistance band.

5 Leg press

Muscles worked: Quadriceps

Reps: 8–12 with each leg for strength, 6–10 with each leg for power
Sets: 1–3
Tempo: 3–1–3 for strength, 1–1–3 for power
Rest: 30–90 seconds between sets

Starting position: Lie on your back on the floor with your knees bent and feet flat on the floor. Raise your left foot off the floor, bringing your knee toward your chest. Loop the band around the arch of your foot and hold an end of the band in each hand with your hands by your knee.

Movement: Extend your leg, pressing your foot away from you. Keep your foot flexed. Hold. Slowly return to the starting position. This is one rep. Finish all reps, then repeat with your right leg. This completes one set.

Tips and techniques:
• Don't lock your knee as you straighten your leg.
• Extend your leg out on a diagonal, not up toward the ceiling.
• Keep your abs tight.

Make it easier: Place your hands closer to the ends of the band for less resistance, or use a lighter resistance band.

Make it harder: Place your hands closer to the center of the band for more resistance, or use a heavier resistance band.

6 Ab crunch with band

Muscles worked: Rectus abdominis, transverse abdominis

Reps: 8–12 for strength, 6–10 for power
Sets: 1–3
Tempo: 3–1–3 for strength, 1–1–3 for power
Rest: 30–90 seconds between sets

Starting position: Anchor a band at a foot or so above floor level (looping it around the leg of a heavy piece of furniture, a railing, or a pole) so you can grasp one end in each hand. Lie on your back on the floor with your head toward the anchor point, your knees bent, and your feet flat on the floor. Bend your arms and position your hands above your face.

Movement: Contract your abdominal muscles and lift your head, shoulders, and upper body off the floor. Hold.

Slowly lower to the starting position.

Tips and techniques:

• Keep your head in line with your spine. Don't point your chin up to the ceiling or down to your chest.

• Exhale as you lift and inhale as you lower.

• Keep your abs tight and tailbone tucked under.

Make it easier: Move closer to the anchor point or adjust your hand position on the band so it has more slack for less resistance, use a lighter resistance band, or do the exercise without a band.

Make it harder: Move farther away from the anchor point or choke up on the band for more resistance, or use a heavier resistance band.

7 Hip extension

Muscles worked: Gluteus

Reps: 8–12 with each leg for strength, 6–10 with each leg for power
Sets: 1–3
Tempo: 3–1–3 for strength, 1–1–3 for power
Rest: 30–90 seconds between sets

Starting position: Anchor a band at a foot or so above floor level (tie it around the leg of a heavy piece of furniture, a railing, or a pole in front of you) and loop the band around your left leg. Stand tall with your feet together. You can lightly hold on to the back of a chair if needed for balance.

Movement: Tighten your abdominal muscles. Tighten your buttocks and raise your left leg directly behind you. Hold. Slowly lower to the starting position. This is one rep. Finish all reps, then repeat with your right leg. This completes one set.

Tips and techniques:

• Keep your hips even and maintain neutral posture.

• Raise your leg directly behind you, not angled out to the side.

• Remain upright as you lift; don't lean your torso forward.

Make it easier: Move closer to the anchor point so the band has more slack for less resistance, use a lighter resistance band, or do the exercise without a band.

Make it harder: Move farther away from the anchor point for more resistance, or use a heavier resistance band.

8 Soccer kick

Muscles worked: Adductors

Reps: 8–12 with each leg for strength, 6–10 with each leg for power
Sets: 1–3
Tempo: 3–1–3 for strength, 1–1–3 for power
Rest: 30–90 seconds between sets

Starting position: Anchor a band near floor level (tie it around the leg of a heavy piece of furniture, a railing, or a pole) and loop it around your left leg. Stand tall with the anchor point on your left and your left foot out to the side. You can lightly hold on to the back of a chair with your left hand if needed for balance.

Movement: Tighten your abdominal muscles. Point your left foot out to the left side, then lift your foot and slowly sweep it diagonally in front of you as if kicking a soccer ball with the inside of your foot. Flex your foot as you swing it. Hold. Slowly bring your foot back to the left side. This is one rep. Finish all reps, then turn around to repeat with the right leg. This completes one set.

Tips and techniques:
• Keep your hips even and maintain neutral posture throughout.
• Tighten your abdominal muscles and the buttock of the standing leg.
• Don't twist your body as you kick.

Make it easier: Move closer to the anchor point so the band has more slack for less resistance, use a lighter resis-

tance band, or do the exercise without a band.

Make it harder: Move farther away from the anchor point for more resistance, or use a heavier resistance band.

9 Side leg lift

Muscles worked: Abductors

Reps: 8–12 with each leg for strength, 6–10 with each leg for power
Sets: 1–3
Tempo: 3–1–3 for strength, 1–1–3 for power
Rest: 30–90 seconds between sets

Starting position: Anchor a band near floor level (tie it around the leg of a heavy piece of furniture, a railing, or a pole) and stand with the anchor point on your left. Loop the band around your right leg so it passes in front of your left leg. Stand tall with your feet together and your hands on your hips. You can lightly hold on to the back of a chair if needed for balance.

Movement: Tighten your abdominal muscles. Slowly raise your right foot out to your right side. Flex your foot as you lift. Hold. Slowly lower back to the starting position. This is one rep. Finish all reps, then turn around to repeat with your left leg. This completes one set.

Tips and techniques:
• Keep your hips even and maintain neutral posture throughout.
• Tighten your abdominal muscles and the buttock of the standing leg.
• Don't lean to the side as you lift.

Make it easier: Move closer to the anchor point so the band has more slack for less resistance, use a lighter resistance band, or do the exercise without a band.

Make it harder: Move farther away from the anchor point for more resistance, or use a heavier resistance band.

QUICK RESISTANCE BAND WORKOUT

On days when you feel that you just don't have time for a full workout, do this abbreviated routine. Some exercise is better than none!

• Chest press (page 28)
• Seated row with rotation (page 29)
• Leg press (page 29)
• Ab crunch with band (page 30)

10 Arm curl

Muscles worked: Biceps

Reps: 8–12 for strength, 6–10 for power

Sets: 1–3

Tempo: 3–1–3 for strength, 1–1–3 for power

Rest: 30–90 seconds between sets

Starting position: Stand on the band, with your feet about shoulder-width apart. Hold an end of the band in each hand with your arms down at your sides, palms facing forward.

Movement: Bend your elbows and raise your hands toward your shoulders. Keep your upper arms stationary and your elbows close to your body. Slowly lower to the starting position.

Tips and techniques:

- Don't move your shoulders or upper arms. The movement is at your elbows.
- Keep your shoulders down and back, away from your ears.
- Keep your wrists straight, in line with your arms.

Make it easier: Place the band under only one foot for more slack and for less resistance.

Make it harder: Place your hands closer to the center of the band for more resistance, or use a heavier resistance band.

11 Arm extension

Muscles worked: Triceps

Reps: 8–12 with each arm for strength, 6–10 with each arm for power

Sets: 1–3

Tempo: 3–1–3 for strength, 1–1–3 for power

Rest: 30–90 seconds between sets

Starting position: Stand tall and hold one end of the band in your right hand. Raise your right arm overhead and bend your elbow, lowering your right hand behind your head with the band hanging behind your back. Bend your left arm behind your lower back so you can grasp the hanging part of the band with your left hand.

Movement: Extend your right arm, raising your right hand overhead. Keep your upper arm stationary and your arm close

to your head. Hold. Slowly lower to the starting position. This is one rep. Finish all reps, then repeat with your left arm. This completes one set.

Tips and techniques:

- Don't move from your shoulder. The movement is at your elbow.
- Keep your shoulders down and back, away from your ears.
- Keep your wrists straight, in line with your arms.

Make it easier: Place your hands farther apart on the band for less resistance, or use a lighter resistance band.

Make it harder: Place your hands closer together on the band for more resistance, or use a heavier resistance band. ▼

YOU'RE NOT DONE YET

See "Stretches," page 46, for a set of eight stretches to end your routine. Stretching helps to prevent stiffness and preserve flexibility and range of motion.

Medicine Ball Workout

You should have some basic strength training under your belt before trying this workout. While you can modify the moves, it is still an advanced routine that combines both strength and power in many of the moves. This makes it a time-efficient workout, but also a more intense one. You may notice that your heart rate goes up more than during other strength workouts.

For a demonstration of the plank pass, go to the video at www.health.harvard.edu/plank-pass.

1 Squat and overhead toss

Muscles worked: Quadriceps, hamstrings, gluteus, pectoralis, deltoids, biceps, rectus abdominis, erector spinae

Reps: 6–10
Sets: 1–3
Tempo: 3–1–1
Rest: 30–90 seconds between sets

Starting position: Stand tall with your feet about shoulder-width apart, toes pointed out slightly. Hold a medicine ball with both hands at chest height, arms bent.

Movement: Bend your hips and knees, and squat down. Don't let your knees move farther forward than your toes. Press into your heels to stand back up. As you rise, toss the ball overhead and catch it, bringing it back to chest height.

Easier

Tips and techniques:
- Keep your chest lifted to avoid leaning too far forward.
- Start with a small toss. Gradually throw the ball higher as you become more comfortable with the exercise.

Make it easier: Do the move without the toss. Instead, simply extend your arms, raising the ball overhead. Use a lighter medicine ball.

Make it harder: Squat lower and extend your arms, touching the ball to the floor, and toss the ball higher. Use a heavier medicine ball.

2 Crunch

Muscles worked: Rectus abdominis, transverse abdominis, pectoralis, deltoids, triceps

Reps: 8–12
Sets: 1–3
Tempo: 3–1–3
Rest: 30–90 seconds between sets

Starting position: Lie faceup on the floor with your legs bent and your feet flat on the floor. Hold a medicine ball close to your chest, elbows angled out to the sides.

Movement: Contract your abdominal muscles and curl your head, shoulders, and upper back off the floor. Simultaneously, extend your arms, thrusting the ball out in front of you. Hold, and then lower.

Tips and techniques:
- Look straight ahead, not up at the ceiling or down at your belly, as you crunch.
- Keep your mid-back on the mat.
- Don't hold your breath.

Make it easier: Hold the ball close to your torso for the entire move. Don't extend your arms. Use a lighter medicine ball.

Make it harder: Hold in the "up" position for three to five seconds. Use a heavier medicine ball.

Easier

3 Overhead floor slam

Muscles worked: Deltoids, latissimus dorsi, rectus abdominis, quadriceps, hamstrings, gluteus, triceps, erector spinae

Reps: 6–10
Sets: 1–3
Tempo: 1–1
Rest: 30–90 seconds between sets

Starting position: Stand tall with your feet about hip-width apart, toes pointing straight ahead. Hold a medicine ball with both hands at chest height, arms bent.

Movement: Extend your arms and bring the ball overhead. In a smooth motion, bring the ball down in front of you as you bend your hips and knees and throw the ball to the floor as hard as possible. Keep your arms straight. Squat down to pick up the ball and return to the starting position.

Tips and techniques:

• Keep your chest lifted.

• Don't bend at your waist.

• Keep your knees no farther forward than your toes.

Make it easier: Instead of slamming the ball to the floor, simply let it drop.

Make it harder: Use a heavier medicine ball.

4 Twist

Muscles worked: Obliques

Reps: 8–12
Sets: 1–3
Tempo: 3–1–3
Rest: 30–90 seconds between sets

Starting position: Stand tall with your feet about hip-width apart, toes pointing straight ahead. Hold a medicine ball with both hands at waist height, arms bent.

Movement: Slowly rotate to the right as far as is comfortable, turning your head to follow. Hold. Return to the center. Rotate to the left. This is one rep.

Tips and techniques:

• Keep your feet flat on the floor.

• Don't rotate your head farther than your arms.

• Keep your abs tight.

Make it easier: Use a lighter medicine ball. Don't rotate as far.

Make it harder: Extend your arms out in front of you and twist. Use a heavier medicine ball.

Harder

5 One-leg dead lift

Muscles worked: Gluteus, hamstrings

Reps: 8–12 with each leg
Sets: 1–3
Tempo: 3–1–3
Rest: 30–90 seconds between sets

Starting position: Stand tall with your feet together, toes pointing straight ahead. Hold a medicine ball with both hands, arms extended down in front of you.

Movement: Shift your weight to your left foot. Slowly raise your right leg behind you as your upper body hinges forward at the hips, lowering the ball toward the floor. Hold. Press into your supporting leg to return to the starting position. Finish all reps, then repeat on the other side. This completes one set.

Easier

Harder

Tips and techniques:
• Keep your hips level.
• Don't lock the knee of your standing leg.
• Lower only until your torso and back leg are parallel to the floor.

Make it easier: Hinge forward only about 45°. Use a lighter medicine ball.

Make it harder: As you stand back up, bring your back leg forward and up into a knee lift before returning to the starting position. Use a heavier medicine ball.

6 Reverse crunch

Muscles worked: Rectus abdominis, transverse abdominis, psoas major, adductors

Reps: 8–12
Sets: 1–3
Tempo: 1–1–2
Rest: 30–90 seconds between sets

Starting position: Lie faceup on the floor with your legs bent and your feet off the floor. Place a medicine ball between your knees, making sure that it is secure. Rest your arms on the floor at your sides, palms down.

Movement: Squeeze the ball with your thighs. Contract your abdominal muscles and lift your buttocks and hips off the floor, bringing your knees toward you. Hold, and then slowly lower. If the ball feels insecure, you can place one hand on it to prevent it from falling on you.

Tips and techniques:
• Keep the movement slow and controlled.
• Don't hold your breath.

Make it easier: Use a lighter medicine ball or none at all.

Make it harder: Hold in the "up" position for three to five seconds. Use a heavier medicine ball.

QUICK MEDICINE BALL WORKOUT

On days when you feel that you just don't have time for a full workout, do this abbreviated routine. Some exercise is better than none!

• Squat and overhead toss (page 33)
• Overhead floor slam (page 34)
• Plank pass (page 36)
• Lunge and lift (page 36)

(7) Plank pass

Muscles worked: Deltoids, biceps, triceps, erector spinae, rectus abdominis, obliques, gluteus, transverse abdominis, quadriceps, hamstrings

Reps: 8–12
Sets: 1–3
Tempo: 1–1
Rest: 30–90 seconds between sets

Starting position: Begin on the floor on all fours with your hands about shoulder-width apart and the medicine ball by your right hand. Lift your knees off the floor and straighten your legs behind you.

Movement: Shift your weight to your left hand so you can place your right hand on the ball. Roll the ball to the left, placing your right hand down and lifting your left hand to stop the ball. Then, roll it to the right. This is one rep.

Tips and techniques:
• Keep your body in line from your head to your heels.

• Keep your abs tight to prevent your back from arching too much.
• Don't drop your head.

Make it easier: Do the move with your knees on the floor. When you've mastered that, lift up into the full plank each time you catch the ball—one hand on the ball and one on the floor. Then, lower your knees to the floor to roll and catch the ball before lifting up into the full plank again. Try holding the full plank a little longer over time until you feel strong enough to do the unmodified move.

Make it harder: Place one foot on top of the other to do the move in a one-leg plank position.

Easier

Harder

(8) Lunge and lift

Muscles worked: Gluteus, quadriceps, hamstrings, triceps

Reps: 8–12
Sets: 1–3
Tempo: 4–1
Rest: 30–90 seconds between sets

Starting position: Stand up straight with your feet together and hold a medicine ball with both hands, with your hands down in front of you.

Movement: Step back onto the ball of your right foot, as you raise the ball over your head. Bend your knees, and lower into a lunge, while simultaneously bending your elbows and lowering the ball behind your head. Your left knee should be over your left foot, and your right knee should point toward the floor. Push off your back foot to stand up, straightening your arms and raising the ball overhead, and return to the starting posi-

tion. Repeat on the opposite side, stepping back with your left foot to do the lunge. This is one rep.

Tips and techniques:
• Keep your spine neutral when lowering into the lunge.
• Don't lean forward or back.
• Keep your shoulders down, away from your ears.

Make it easier: Use a lighter medicine ball. Another option is to do stationary lunges instead of stepping back and forth: Stand with one foot in front of the other and lower into the lunge. Finish all reps, then switch legs and repeat for one set.

Make it harder: Step forward into the lunge instead of backward, and as you stand back up do a knee lift. Use a heavier medicine ball. 🔻

YOU'RE NOT DONE YET

See "Stretches," page 46, for a set of eight stretches to end your routine. Stretching helps to prevent stiffness and preserve flexibility and range of motion.

Kettlebell Workout

Get ready for a trio of benefits from the Kettlebell Workout. Like the Medicine Ball Workout, this routine contains more advanced moves that build both strength and power. But you'll also get a heart-pumping cardio workout because of the vigorous actions of many of the exercises. It is important that you practice these moves without a kettlebell at first, so that you learn good technique to avoid injury. You should also start by doing the moves at a slower tempo and gradually progress to the paces noted in the exercise instructions.

For further advice on how to perform kettlebell exercises properly, getting maximum benefits while minimizing your risk of injury, go to the video at www.health.harvard.edu/kettlebell.

1 Basic swing

Muscles worked: Deltoids, erector spinae, rectus abdominis, gluteus, quadriceps, hamstrings

Reps: 8–12
Sets: 1–3
Tempo: 1–1
Rest: 30–90 seconds between sets

Starting position: Stand tall with your feet about shoulder-width apart. Hold a kettlebell with both hands, arms extended down in front of you so the kettlebell hangs between your legs.

Movement: Hinge forward at your hips, shift your weight onto your heels, and sit back, swinging the kettlebell back between your legs. Then press into your heels and stand up as you swing the kettlebell forward to chest height.

Tips and techniques:
- Keep your abs tight.
- Don't round your back or bend at the waist.
- Don't push your hips out in front of your body or lean back as you stand up.

Make it easier: Use a lighter kettlebell.

Make it harder: Hold the kettlebell in one hand and pass it to the other at the high point of each swing.

Harder

② Halo

Muscles worked: Rectus abdominis, obliques, transverse abdominis, deltoids, erector spinae

Reps: 8–12
Sets: 1–3
Tempo: 3
Rest: 30–90 seconds between sets

Starting position: Stand with your feet about shoulder-width apart. Hold a kettlebell with both hands so it is over and behind your head.

Movement: Circle the kettlebell clockwise over your head for half of the repetitions. Then circle counterclockwise for the remaining repetitions. This completes one set.

Tips and techniques:
• Keep your lower body stationary.
• Don't pull your shoulders up toward your ears; keep them down and back.
• Keep your abs tight.

Make it easier: Make smaller circles, or use a lighter kettlebell.

Make it harder: Make larger circles, or use a heavier kettlebell.

③ High pull

Muscles worked: Gluteus, quadriceps, hamstrings, deltoids, biceps

Reps: 8–12
Sets: 1–3
Tempo: 3–1–3–1 for strength, 1–1–1–1 for power
Rest: 30–90 seconds between sets

Starting position: Stand with your feet more than shoulder-width apart and your toes pointing slightly out to the sides. Hold a kettlebell with both hands down in front of you.

Movement: Bend your knees, lowering into a plié squat. Hold. As you stand up, bend your elbows out to the sides and pull the kettlebell up to about chest height. Hold again. This is one rep.

Make it easier: Do the pull without squatting.

Make it harder: Hold the kettlebell in one hand only and do the pulls with one arm at a time.

Tips and techniques:
• Don't let your knees roll in as you squat.
• Keep your abs tight.
• Your knees should be over your ankles.

Harder

④ Lunge press

Muscles worked: Deltoids, triceps, obliques, gluteus, quadriceps, hamstrings

Reps: 8–12
Sets: 1–3
Tempo: 3–1–3 for strength, 2–1–1 for power
Rest: 30–90 seconds between sets

Starting position: Stand with your feet together and hold a kettlebell with both hands by your chest.

Movement: Step back onto the ball of your left foot, bend your knees, and lower into a lunge. At the same time, extend your arms and press the kettlebell overhead. Your right knee should align over your right ankle, and your left knee should point toward (but not touch) the floor. Hold. Push off your back foot to stand up and return to the starting position. Repeat, stepping back with your right foot to do the lunge on the opposite side. This is one rep.

Tips and techniques:
- Keep your spine neutral when lowering into the lunge.
- Don't lean forward or back.
- As you bend your knees, lower the back knee directly down toward the floor, with the thigh perpendicular to the floor.

Harder

Make it easier: Do the lunge without pressing the kettlebell overhead.

Make it harder: Hold the kettlebell in one hand to do the presses with one arm at a time.

⑤ Windmill

Muscles worked: Obliques, erector spinae, rectus abdominis

Reps: 8–12 on each side
Sets: 1–3
Tempo: 3–1–3 for strength, 3–1–1 for power
Rest: 30–90 seconds between sets

Starting position: Stand tall with your feet more than shoulder-width apart. Hold a kettlebell in your left hand with your left arm extended overhead, and your right arm down at your side.

Movement: Slowly bend to your right side as far as is comfortable. Let your right hand slide down your right leg as you bend. Look up at your left hand. Hold. Slowly return to the starting position. Finish all reps, then repeat on the opposite side. This completes one set.

Tips and techniques:
- Don't let your body roll forward as you bend.
- Keep your abs tight.
- Don't twist your neck too far.

Make it easier: Hold the kettlebell in your other hand, down at your side, instead of over your head.

Make it harder: Hold a kettlebell in each hand.

Easier

QUICK KETTLEBELL WORKOUT

On days when you feel that you just don't have time for a full workout, do this abbreviated routine. Some exercise is better than none!

- Basic swing (page 37)
- High pull (page 38)
- Seated twist (page 40)
- Get up (page 41)

6 Figure 8

Muscles worked: Deltoids, erector spinae, rectus abdominis, obliques

Reps: 8–12 in each direction
Sets: 1–3
Tempo: 1–1–1–1
Rest: 30–90 seconds between sets

Starting position: Stand tall with your feet more than shoulder-width apart. Hold a kettlebell in your right hand with your right arm at your side.

Movement: Bend your knees and bring the kettlebell around the front of your right leg and pass it between your legs to your left hand. Straighten up as you

Easier

bring the kettlebell around in front of your left leg, and squat again to pass it between your legs back to your right hand. This is one rep. Finish all reps, then

repeat going in the opposite direction. This completes one set.

Tips and techniques:
• Keep your abs tight.
• Be careful that you don't hit your legs as you pass the kettlebell between them.
• Maintain control.

Make it easier: Circle the kettlebell around your waist. Or, use a lighter kettlebell.

Make it harder: Use a heavier kettlebell, or squat lower.

7 Seated twist

Muscles worked: Rectus abdominis, obliques, transverse abdominis, erector spinae

Reps: 8–12
Sets: 1–3
Tempo: 2–2–2–2 for strength, 1–1–1–1 for power
Rest: 30–90 seconds between sets

Starting position: Sit on the floor with your knees bent and feet on the floor. Hold a kettlebell with both hands in front of your chest. Shift your weight onto your tailbone and raise your feet off the floor.

Movement: Slowly twist to the left. Hold. Return to the center, and then twist to the right. This is one rep.

Tips and techniques:
• Keep your chest lifted.
• Don't lean back too far.
• Don't hold your breath.

Make it easier: Keep your heels on the floor. Use a lighter kettlebell.

Make it harder: Raise your feet higher off the floor. Use a heavier kettlebell.

Easier

8 Get up

Muscles worked: Pectoralis, triceps, deltoids, erector spinae, rectus abdominis, gluteus, quadriceps, hamstrings

Reps: 4–6 on each side
Sets: 1–3
Tempo: 1–1–1–1–1
Rest: 30–90 seconds between sets

Starting position: Lie faceup on the floor with your right leg bent, foot flat on the floor, and your left leg extended. Hold a kettlebell in your right hand with your right arm bent, elbow pointing out to the side and upper arm resting on the floor.

Movement: Extend your right arm, pressing the kettlebell straight up to the ceiling. Curl your head and torso off the floor, rising up onto your left elbow and forearm. Shift onto your left hand, sitting up further. Shift your weight onto your right foot and slide your left leg back and under your torso, rising up onto your left knee. Press into your right foot to stand up, bringing your feet together. Hold, and then slowly reverse the moves, returning to the starting position. Complete all reps on one side, then repeat with the opposite arm and leg.

Tips and techniques:
• Exhale as you exert effort.
• Keep your abs tight.
• Maintain control.

Make it easier: Rise only to the seated position.

Make it harder: Try using a heavier kettlebell. ▼

YOU'RE NOT DONE YET

See "Stretches," page 46, for a set of eight stretches to end your routine. Stretching helps to prevent stiffness and preserve flexibility and range of motion.

Bonus power moves: Plyometrics

Adding a few of these jump moves to any strength workout that you do will boost your power by training your fast-twitch muscle fibers (see "Slow-twitch and fast-twitch fibers," page 7), the nerves that activate them, and your reflexes. If you have never done plyometrics, start with the beginner moves. Even if you have some experience with this type of exercise, that's still a good place to start, and then you can progress to the other levels more quickly.

Perform plyometrics at the beginning of your training session—but *after* you are warmed up. Do three sets of five reps for each move, allowing at least a minute of rest in between sets. If this is too much for you, you can do fewer reps or sets. Over time, gradually work up to 15 reps per set. Aim to do plyometrics one to three times a week, allowing 48 to 72 hours in between sessions for adequate recovery. When you are ready for a new challenge, try the next level of jumps, starting with three sets of five reps and progressing from there.

Here are some tips to maximize your efforts while minimizing your risk for injury:

- Choose a surface with some give. A thick, firm mat (not the yoga kind); well-padded, carpeted wood floor; or grass or dirt, outside, are good choices that absorb some of the impact. Do not jump on tile, concrete, or asphalt surfaces. These have no "give" in them and can lead to shin splints.
- Jump slowly in the beginning. The faster you jump, the more intense the workout.
- Aim for just a few inches off the floor to start. The higher you jump, the greater your impact on landing.
- Bend your legs when you land. Don't lock your knees.
- Land softly on your midfoot, not your heels or balls of your feet.
- Drop your hips as you land to absorb some of the impact.
- Engage your core muscles to protect your spine.
- Lean slightly forward, with your head up and your torso rigid (chest over knees, nose over toes) as you land.
- If you have had any joint issues, especially in your knees, back, or hips, check with your doctor before doing any plyometric training.

BEGINNER: Knee hops

Muscles worked: Gluteus, quadriceps, hamstrings, gastrocnemius

Reps: 5–15 with each leg
Sets: 1–3
Rest: 1–3 minutes between sets

Starting position: Stand tall with your feet together.

Movement: Raise your left knee up to about hip height, hopping a little bit off the floor with your right foot as you lift. Immediately repeat with your opposite leg. Continue alternating legs. Let your arms swing naturally.

Tips and techniques:
- Don't hunch or round your shoulders forward.
- Keep your abs tight.

Make it easier: Don't lift your knee as high. Don't hop as high, or keep your toes on the floor as you raise your heel.

Make it harder: Lift your knee higher. Hop higher.

BEGINNER: Side hops

Muscles worked: Gluteus, abductors, adductors, quadriceps, hamstrings, gastrocnemius

Reps: 5–15 to each side
Sets: 1–3
Rest: 1–3 minutes between sets

Starting position: Stand tall with your feet together.

Movement: Shift your weight onto your right foot and leap to your left, landing with your left foot, followed by your right one. Repeat, hopping to your right. You can hold your arms in front of you or let them swing naturally.

Tips and techniques:
• Don't hunch or round your shoulders forward.
• Keep your abs tight.

Make it easier: Hop a shorter distance to the side and stay lower to the floor.

Make it harder: Make your hops bigger and higher.

INTERMEDIATE: Forward and backward hops

Muscles worked: Gluteus, quadriceps, hamstrings, gastrocnemius

Reps: 5–15
Sets: 1–3
Rest: 1–3 minutes between sets

Starting position: Stand tall with your feet together.

Movement: Bend your knees and jump forward one to two feet. Then jump back to the starting position. Let your arms swing naturally.

Tips and techniques:
• Don't hunch or round your shoulders forward.
• Keep your abs tight.

Make it easier: Hop a shorter distance and stay lower to the floor.

Make it harder: Make your hops longer and higher.

INTERMEDIATE: Jumping jacks

Muscles worked: Deltoids, gluteus, quadriceps, hamstrings, gastrocnemius

Reps: 5–15
Sets: 1–3
Rest: 1–3 minutes between sets

Starting position: Stand tall with your feet together, arms at your sides.

Movement: Jump and spread your feet apart, more than shoulder-width, as you raise your arms out to the sides and over your head. Jump and bring your feet back together, bringing your arms down to your sides. This is one rep.

Tips and techniques:
• Don't hunch or round your shoulders forward.
• Keep your abs tight.
• Keep your shoulders down and back, away from your ears.

Make it easier: Don't move your feet as far apart, and stay lower to the floor.

Make it harder: Make your jumps higher and faster.

ADVANCED: Lateral jumps

Muscles worked: Gluteus, abductors, quadriceps, hamstrings, gastrocnemius

Reps: 5–15
Sets: 1–3
Rest: 1–3 minutes between sets

Starting position: Stand tall with your feet together, arms at your sides.

Movement: Bend your knees and jump to your left with both feet. Then jump back to the starting position. This is one rep.

Tips and techniques:
• Don't hunch or round your shoulders forward.
• Keep your abs tight.

Make it easier: Jump a shorter distance and stay lower to the floor.

Make it harder: Make your jumps longer, higher, or faster.

ADVANCED: Burpees

Muscles worked: Deltoids, pectoralis, rectus abdominis, transverse abdominis, erector spinae, gluteus, quadriceps, hamstrings, gastrocnemius

Reps: 5–15
Sets: 1–3
Rest: 1–3 minutes between sets

Starting position: Stand tall with your feet together, arms at your sides.

Movement: Squat down placing your hands on the floor. Jump your legs back behind you into plank position. Jump your feet back in toward your hands. Jump up into the air, landing in the starting position. This is one rep.

Tips and techniques:
• Keep your head and neck in line with your spine.
• Keep your abs tight.

Make it easier: Walk your feet in and out of the plank position instead of jumping. Don't jump as high.

Make it harder: Make your jump higher. Move more quickly from one position to the next. ◗

Stretches

Stretching is an important, if frequently overlooked, part of a routine. When done correctly, stretching helps loosen tight muscles, keeping you more limber. It also gives you a greater, more comfortable range of motion and improves posture and balance. A good time to stretch is after exercising, as part of your cool-down session, because that is when muscles are most pliable. Stretching during your workout is fine, too, and may help boost flexibility, so if you prefer, you can do a stretch or two after each exercise once your muscles are warmed up.

For optimal results, hold each stretch for 10 to 30 seconds, then repeat it until you reach a total of 60 seconds. If you hold the position for less time or do fewer repetitions, you won't lengthen the muscle fibers as effectively. On the other hand, holding a stretch for too long can increase your chances of injuring the muscle. When you are starting out, you may find that it's useful to time your stretches.

Here are some other safety tips:
- While stretching, remember to breathe normally.
- Don't bounce.
- Don't overextend your body. Stretch only to the point of mild tension, never pain. If a stretch hurts, stop immediately.

If you have had a joint replaced or repaired, ask your surgeon whether you need to avoid certain stretches, such as the torso rotation. If you have osteoporosis, consult your doctor before doing floor stretches or stretches that bend the spine.

1 Chest opener

Where you'll feel it: Chest and shoulders

Reps: 2–6
Hold: 10–30 seconds

Starting position: Stand with your feet together and your arms at your sides.

Movement: Clasp your hands together behind you. Gently raise your hands as high as is comfortable, pulling your shoulders back and opening up your chest. Hold. Return to the starting position.

Tips and techniques:
- If you have difficulty clasping your hands, hold on to a towel or strap with both hands.
- Keep your shoulders down and back.
- Don't lean forward or excessively arch your back.

2 Triceps stretch

Where you'll feel it: Back of upper arm

Reps: 2–6
Hold: 10–30 seconds

Starting position: Stand with your feet comfortably apart and your arms at your sides.

Movement: Raise your right arm overhead and bend your elbow so your right hand is behind your head. Place your left hand on your right elbow and gently pull it toward the left. Hold. Slowly return to the starting position. Repeat with your left arm behind your head. This is one rep.

Tips and techniques:
- Keep your chest lifted and your eyes straight ahead.
- Keep your back straight and your shoulders down and back.
- Don't lean to the side.

3 Calf stretch

Where you'll feel it: Back of lower leg, ankle, top of thigh

Reps: 2–6
Hold: 10–30 seconds

Starting position: Stand up straight with your feet together and your hands on your hips or down at your sides.

Movement: Step with your left foot 12 to 24 inches behind you and bend your right knee. Keeping both feet flat, press your left heel against the floor as you lean forward from the ankle. Hold. Return to the starting position, then repeat with your right leg back. This is one rep.

Tips and techniques:
• Keep your toes pointing forward.
• Your hips and shoulders should remain squared, facing forward.
• If you don't feel a stretch, place your foot farther back.

4 Quadriceps stretch

Where you'll feel it: Front of thigh

Reps: 2–6
Hold: 10–30 seconds

Starting position: Stand with your feet together. Place your right hand on the back of a chair for balance if needed.

Movement: Bend your left knee and bring your heel toward your left buttock. Grasp your left foot with your left hand. Hold. Slowly return to the starting position. Repeat on the other side. This is one rep.

Tips and techniques:
• Don't grasp your toes.
• If you have trouble reaching your foot, loop a strap or belt around your ankle and gently pull the strap toward your buttocks.
• Don't arch your back.
• Make sure your bent knee is pointing straight down toward the floor.
• Tuck your tailbone under to feel a deeper stretch.

5 Knees to chest

Where you'll feel it: Lower and middle back, hips

Reps: 2–6
Hold: 10–30 seconds

Starting position: Lie on your back with your legs extended on the floor. Rest your arms at your sides.

Movement: Bend both knees and grasp the backs of your thighs with your hands, pulling your knees in toward your chest. Hold. Return to the starting position.

Tips and techniques:
• Bring your chin to your chest for a greater stretch.
• When holding the stretch, remain as still as possible.

6 Figure-4 stretch

Where you'll feel it: Buttocks, hip, and outer thigh

Reps: 2–6
Hold: 10–30 seconds

Starting position: Lie on your back on the floor with your knees bent and your feet flat.

Movement: Place your left ankle across your right thigh just above the knee. Grasp your right leg behind the thigh and gently pull it in toward your chest until you feel mild tension in your left hip and buttock. Hold. Slowly return to the starting position. Repeat with your right ankle across your left thigh. This is one rep.

Tips and techniques:
• Keep your head on the floor.
• Keep your hips squared; don't let them roll to one side.
• For a deeper stretch, use your hand to press your bent leg away from you.

7 Torso rotation*

Where you'll feel it: Back, chest, and outer thigh

Reps: 2–6
Hold: 10–30 seconds

Starting position:
Lie on your back with
your knees bent and
feet together, flat on
the floor. Extend your
arms out comfort-
ably to each side at
shoulder level, palms down.

Movement: Tighten your abdominal muscles and slowly
lower your knees to the right side, keeping them together and
resting them on the floor. Keep your shoulders relaxed and
pressed against the floor as you turn your head in the opposite direction, looking toward your left hand. You can place
your right hand on your left thigh to deepen the stretch. Hold.
Return to the starting position. Repeat in the opposite direction. This is one rep.

Tips and techniques:
- When holding the stretch, remain as still as possible, without
  bouncing.
- If it's too difficult to rest your knees on the floor, place a
  folded blanket on the floor and rest them on it.
- If necessary, put a rolled towel between your knees to make
  this stretch easier.

*If you have had a hip replacement, talk to your doctor before
trying this stretch. It may be best for you to avoid it.*

8 Hamstring stretch

Where you'll feel it: Back of thigh

Reps: 2–6
Hold: 10–30 seconds

Starting position: Lie on your back on the floor with your
legs extended. Loop a strap or belt around your right foot and
grasp the ends.

Movement: Raise your right leg off the floor as high as possible. Then gently pull on the strap to bring your right leg in
toward your chest as far as you comfortably can. Hold. Slowly
return to the starting position. Repeat with your left leg. This
is one rep.

Tips and techniques:
- Keep your legs straight, but don't lock your knees.
- If you don't have a strap or you prefer not to use one, you
  can grasp the back of your thigh with both hands.
- If you feel any strain or are unable to maintain good form,
  you can bend the opposite leg and place that foot flat on
  the floor. ◆

Taking it to the next level

The workouts in this report are a good place to start when it comes to building strength and power. But at some point, you will likely want to switch up your routine to prevent boredom and ensure that you keep seeing results. Variety adds spice to all parts of life, and working out is no different. Here are some ways to keep you motivated, so you keep making progress.

Try a weighted vest

A simple way to increase the challenge is to slip on a weighted vest and do your usual workouts. A weighted vest can add additional resistance for stationary moves such as bridges and planks. For moving exercises such as lunges or plyometrics, a weighted vest will help you develop more power.

If you want to wear a weighted vest, choose one with removable weights in half-pound to 1-pound bars. You can find vests online by searching for "weighted vest," or you may be able to find them at a department store, discount store, or sporting goods store. Prices range from about $30 to more than $200. (The more weight it holds, the more expensive it tends to be.)

Follow the guidelines in Table 2 (page 50) to determine how much weight to start with, the amount to add every one to two weeks, and the maximum amount of weight to use. For example, a 150-pound woman would add 3 pounds to her vest every week or two. Over the course of about six to 12 weeks, the weight would increase as follows: 3 pounds, 6 pounds, 9 pounds, 12 pounds, 15 pounds, and finally 18 pounds. She should not put more than 18 pounds into her vest.

If your workout feels too vigorous at any time or if you can't complete the recommended two to three sets of an exercise with the vest on, reduce the amount of weight in your vest to a more comfortable level.

Join a gym

A gym can provide a lot of new options for working out. It offers a change of scenery, companionship with other exercisers, and a wide range of equipment and classes to keep you challenged and engaged with working out. While you can certainly work out at home with resistance bands and hand weights, a gym is likely to offer a broad range of heavy machines that you wouldn't buy for your home. Plus, spending money on a gym mem-

A gym can provide a lot of new options for working out. If can offer a range of equipment too large for your home and may also provide classes to keep your workouts interesting.

Table 2: Guidelines for adding weight to your vest

IF YOU WEIGH	STARTING WEIGHT; increase the weight in your vest every one to two weeks by this amount	MAXIMUM AMOUNT TO USE IN YOUR VEST
75–99 pounds	1 pound	7 pounds
100–149 pounds	2 pounds	12 pounds
150–199 pounds	3 pounds	18 pounds
200–239 pounds	4 pounds	20 pounds
240–280 pounds	5 pounds	25 pounds
281–329 pounds	6 pounds	30 pounds
330 pounds or more	7 pounds	35 pounds

bership can motivate you to go to the gym to get your money's worth.

Before deciding whether a gym is right for you, consider your preferences and needs. Ask yourself some questions: How far must you travel to the gym, and are you likely to make the trek? Do the gym's hours of operation work well for you? Consider what amenities you are likely to use—classes, trainers, or just equipment—and look for a facility that offers what you want rather than a lot of extras you don't need. High-end gyms with a lot of classes, fancy locker rooms, and juice bars can cost several hundred dollars a month in major metropolitan areas. Low-end gyms that just offer equipment can cost as little as $10 a month, so it pays to shop around. Some gyms also offer different levels of membership with different perks, so you may not have to pay for services you won't use.

Get expert help

A personal trainer can be your biggest cheerleader—and once you've paid for a session, you're definitely going to show up. Some of the most valuable skills trainers bring are teaching you new skills, helping you change up your routines to beat boredom, and safely pushing you to the next level. They can also tailor an exercise program to any goals you choose: enhancing health and appearance, losing weight, charging through a triathlon, or another aim entirely.

However, not all trainers are equally good. If you are older, for example, young trainers may try to push you too far too fast, urging you to try things that are fine for kids in their 20s, but risky for people in their 50s, 60s, or beyond. Ask the gym if a particular trainer is used to dealing with people your age or with your limitations. No nationwide licensing requirements exist for personal trainers. So in addition to seeking a good match in personalities and respect for your goals, you should ask about these points:

Certification. Certifying organizations include the American College of Sports Medicine (ACSM), American Council on Exercise (ACE), National Academy of Sports Medicine (NASM), and other groups whose certifications are recognized by the National Commission for Certifying Agencies (NCCA).

Experience. Years of experience matter, as does experience in working with others like you, whether you're a gifted athlete or a

A personal trainer can teach you new skills and help keep you motivated. But, if you're older, try to find one who is used to working with people your age.

© andresr | Getty Images

Heavy ropes, also known as battle ropes, provide an interesting and novel way to build upper-body strength.

confirmed sloth with tricky knees. Some trainers specialize in working with particular populations—older adults, athletes, pregnant women, cancer survivors—and may have taken courses and possibly certifying exams in these areas.

References. Ask health care providers such as doctors, physical therapists, chiropractors, massage therapists, dietitians, and friends for referrals. Certifying organizations like ACE and ACSM often have referral systems. Before signing on with a trainer, ask for references and call a few.

Liability insurance. Whether a trainer works for a gym or independently, make sure he or she has liability insurance.

Take a class

Most of the time when you think of an exercise class, cardio comes to mind, but now there is an array of classes that include strength training, power training, or both. And you don't have to join a gym or

studio to give it a try. You can find a range of on-demand classes on your smartphone, tablet, or smart TV. These allow you to work out on your own and still participate in a class. The options include everything from boot camp and high-intensity interval training to yoga. Many services like Daily Burn and Peloton Digital (no bike required) offer livestreamed classes as well as recorded ones. While there is a fee for these services, it may be less than a gym or studio membership, and you don't have to drive anywhere. Some offer free 30-day trial periods, so you can test them out first.

Here are some classes to try that will amp up your strength, power, or both, and you're likely to get cardio or flexibility benefits, too.

Barre classes. Exercises are performed at a ballet barre and focus on strengthening individual muscle groups while improving flexibility, posture, and balance. No power training here.

BodyPump / body sculpting classes. Group strength training workouts are set to music to make lifting weights more fun. The focus tends to be on using light weights for many repetitions to build endurance. Some strength benefits may be possible depending on your fitness level.

Boot camps. These military-inspired workouts, done outdoors or indoors, get your heart pumping for cardio benefits and work your muscles for both strength and power gains.

CrossFit. A regimen of high-intensity interval training provides cardio, strength, and power training. Because of its vigorous nature (flipping tires and hefting very heavy weights), proceed with caution if you decide to try it.

Heavy ropes (battle ropes). More and more gyms are offering giant-sized ropes, attached to an anchor point, as a novel way to build upper-body strength and power. Depending on the moves you do, you could also get a bit of a cardio workout.

Indoor rock climbing. Most people think of climbing as an upper-body activity, but in reality, it's a full-body strength workout that challenges your brain as you try to figure out the best route up the wall. Climb quickly and you'll also get a cardio workout, and reaching for holds challenges your flexibility.

Kickboxing is primarily a type of aerobic exercise, but its swift punches also help develop power.

Competitive obstacle-course training, such as Ninja Warrior or Tough Mudder, offers a hard-core workout.

Kickboxing/boxing. Punching and kicking during this high-energy cardio workout helps to build power. It can improve speed and agility, which are components of power, but it doesn't offer much in the way of strength training.

Martial arts. High-energy styles of martial arts with jumps, kicks, and blocks can provide cardio, strength, and power benefits. Most classes also include stretching for a well-rounded workout.

Ninja Warrior or Tough Mudder workouts. As obstacle-course-style races have gained popularity, workouts to train for them have popped up. These hard-core workouts generally hit all the fitness components—cardio, strength, power, flexibility—with an emphasis on strength.

Pilates. Pilates is the quintessential workout for developing core strength. Equipment can include weighted hand balls, resistance bands or straps, and machines with pulleys, cables, and straps for resistance. But even Pilates classes done on a mat with no equipment can help you get stronger. No cardio or power benefits, however.

Pound. This is a drumming-inspired, full-body cardio and strength workout with some Pilates and yoga. Using lightly weighted drumsticks called Ripstix, you tap the sticks together and drum on the floor while squatting, lunging, and performing core moves like bridges and boat pose. And all that pounding is a great way to work off stress.

Spin or indoor cycling. While it looks like it's all cardio, you'll get some strength training, too. This group workout on stationary bikes toggles between heart-pumping vigorous intervals and catch-your-breath recovery intervals. Throughout, your core muscles will be engaged to keep you upright, especially when you hop out of the saddle. You can also increase resistance as you pedal to really challenge your lower-body muscles.

Step aerobics. Hopping and stepping up and down during this cardio workout can provide some lower-body strength gains. And the more hopping and jumping over the step you do, the more power training you'll get.

TRX. This unique bodyweight workout uses straps that are anchored overhead to suspend you as you do the exercises. It's a strength workout that really works your core. Some moves may also provide power benefits.

Water workouts. Water provides resistance, so you get both cardio and strength benefits when you hop in the pool. And if you're doing moves like running and jumping, you may also get some power benefits.

Yoga. Holding poses helps to build strength and muscle endurance, while flowing stretches increase flexibility. Some vigorous styles of yoga, such as Ashtanga, may provide some cardio benefits. ▼

TRX uses straps that are anchored overhead to suspend you as you do the exercises. It's a strength workout that is especially good for your core, but some moves provide power, too.

Children of the Seventh Fire: An Ancient Prophecy for Modern Times

Big Oak Publishing
Glenford, New York
www.childrenoftheseventhfire.com

Printed in Canada by Friesens, Altona, Manitoba, with the use of vegetable-based inks, FSC-certified sustainably harvested paper, and other environmentally sensitive practices.

Library of Congress Control Number: 2021907223

ISBN 978-0-578-89302-0 Softcover
ISBN 978-0-578-88560-5 Hardcover

Children of the Seventh Fire

An Ancient Prophecy for Modern Times

by
Lisa A. Hart

illustrated by
Joe Liles

Foreword by
Edward Benton-Banai

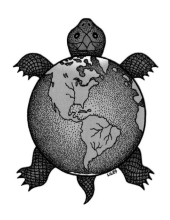

Big Oak Publishing
Glenford, New York

Table of Contents

Foreword

I have memories about a book from grade school days. It was called *History of America*. It was about the people who migrated to America from lands far across the ocean to search for a better life. I and other students of a Wisconsin public school which was ninety percent Native American were ordered to read, study, and write papers based upon this book. We read chapter after chapter, memorizing the names of wondrous immigrant heroes and their exploits in war and exploration. The book contained stories and drawings of men who had carved out a nation among the savages of what they saw as a new, empty land.

These portrayals, however, were false, but they have remained in the history books of public and parochial schools for a long time. It was difficult for me, a nine-year-old full-blood Ojibwe boy, to read this incomplete version of history day after day and be expected to believe it. 1492, the year that the European sailor Christopher Columbus first reached the Americas, is a date embedded in my memory. For me and other Native Americans, however, Columbus' arrival was not very wondrous.

I and my classmates wanted to read about the prominent men and women of the great Ojibwe Nation, the Six Nations, and other tribes. Where were the accounts of the accomplishments of our native leaders like Tecumseh, Handsome Lake, Shingwaukoons, Quannah Parker, or Sitting Bull? Sacajawea was the only native woman mentioned. We didn't make it into the history books in a positive way, perhaps because what we were reading was HIS STORY only. It seemed that Indian people were not part of the American story, at least, according to *History of America*. In fact, however, Native Americans of every tribe and nation are a part of America's history and the fabric of human kind. The tracks and artifacts of native people are recorded and dated far back, perhaps to as much as 50,000 years ago.

Fortunately, since the 1970s, some things have changed for the better. Although the books of today still often contain much of the biased and incomplete information from the past, more and more often these books contain parts of OUR STORY, the long and rich story of Native Americans.

Lisa Hart — writer, educator, caring human being — is one person who is helping to tell our story. Her very well written book, *Children of the Seventh Fire*, illustrated by renowned artist Joe Liles, introduces school children of today to an important element of Native American heritage. The children in the story take the reader to a strange but exciting place — an Indian reservation. And there, in a lodge, the reader meets an Indian man who is a teacher, a storyteller. His name is Gikinoo Amaagaydnini, "He Who Teaches You," and he wears a turban made of otter skin, a tradition among the men of the ancient Midewiwin Society. His message reveals the Seven Prophecies of the Anishinabe and places this valued piece of oral tradition into a modern context in a way that can be understood, experienced, and of benefit to all who come to know and understand it.

I give this book and the author my unconditional support. As my 10-year-old granddaughter has pronounced, "The book is very cool." Cool indeed. Excellent!

Mi'gwetch — thank you for the privilege.

Bawdwaywidun Banaise, a.k.a. Eddie Benton-Banai, B.S. History, MBA; Grand Chief, Three Fires Midewiwin Society; Faculty, Shingwauk, Imminent University

Chapter 1

Down a Bumpy Road

The school bus pulled up to the front entrance of the elementary school and the bus driver opened the door. Just before the students boarded, Mrs.Tomlin stopped them and said some words of warning. "We're going to the Birch River Reservation to hear an Ojibwe *(Oh-**jib**-way)* elder share an ancient story with us — so remember, you are expected to act in a respectful manner."

"Oh my goodness," thought Kayla, looking towards TJ at the back of the line. "I hope he doesn't embarrass us all by saying something mean to the elder we're going to see and I hope he's forgot that I'm part Ojibwe. I really don't feel like being teased all the way there."

Just then, TJ let out a "Woo-woo, woo-woo, woo-woo!" Looking toward the back of the line, Mrs. Tomlin said sternly, "TJ, that will be enough! We will have none of that on this trip or on these school grounds."

"It's going to be a long day!" Kayla thought, rolling her eyes.

Kayla had lived next door to TJ until last year, when her father sold the farm and they moved into the large town of Johnston, nearby. TJ's parents were still trying to hold onto their farm, and they struggled financially to keep it going. TJ and Kayla had spent many years playing in the shallow creeks, grassy hills, and woods on the two farms. They had stretched their imaginations to the fullest, making up fantasy stories and then playing the main characters. They were very best friends! Then, when they were about eight, TJ changed. Something happened to him. He became mean, sometimes even to Kayla.

Every morning TJ had several hours of chores to do before he went to school. His classmates teased him when he came to school with cow manure and mud on his shoes, even though he tried to clean them off the best he could. Kayla suspected that being teased so much was what had changed him. It was sad, because she missed his friendship so much. Now that she no longer lived on the farm next door, it seemed that they would never have anything in common again.

After driving a couple of hours north on the Interstate, the bus exited and turned down a series of long roads, turning left, then right, then right again at a sign that read, "You Are Now Entering Birch River Indian Reservation." A little farther on, they passed under an old train trestle with a graffiti message that read, "THIS IS INDIAN LAND!"

Kayla noticed something looked different. The trees were taller and larger than most she had seen. The forest seemed healthier. It was a glaring contrast to the acres and acres of clear-cut countryside she had seen along the way. Here on the reservation, the forest had been left intact. Kayla didn't think she had ever seen a more beautiful forest. As a matter of fact, she thought that this might be the first time she had ever seen a *real* forest!

Making a final turn, the bus veered to the left. It bumped and jerked down a long dirt road that seemed to go on for miles. "Where on Earth are we going?" Kayla wondered.

The bus came to a halt at the edge of a clearing in the forest. There, in the middle of the clearing, was a long domed structure, with brown tarps covering it.

"That must be the teaching lodge of the Three Fires Midewiwin *(Mih-**day**-win)* Lodge Mrs. Tomlin told us about," thought Kayla. She could see smoke gently lifting up through a hole in the middle of the lodge roof. "I hope we're going to sit in there. It will be a real campfire story! Nobody has real campfires anymore, at least not in town where I live. This is going to be awesome!" Kayla imagined.

After Kayla and her classmates scrambled out of the bus, Kayla looked around and noticed another bunch of kids her age quietly talking and playing in the shade of the white birch, maple, and pine trees at the edge of the clearing. They looked like they might be from the reservation elementary school. "They must have come to hear the elder, too," Kayla thought.

To the right was a cliff overlooking Lake Superior. "How beautiful the view is, across the endless deep-blue shimmering water," Kayla thought. A fresh spring breeze blew up the cliff and into her hair.

Kayla and her classmates stood a safe distance from the cliff and talked excitedly amongst themselves. Kayla was a little embarrassed that a group of boys was being loud, and as always TJ was the loudest one of them all. Of course! What did she expect?

Everyone stopped talking abruptly when they heard a piercing *screeeeeeeech* coming from the sky just above. They looked up and there it was! Above their heads was a large bald eagle, circling far up in the blue sky! Even the boys who had been horsing around stopped and looked up. A minute or two passed while all eyes were fixed on the majestic bird until, finally, the eagle soared off toward the western horizon of the great lake.

The last of the still silence was interrupted by a booming voice that called from the doorway at the end of the lodge.

"Boozhoo *(boo-**jhoo**)*!" said the man.

Everyone jumped a little and turned their heads all at once to see who it was. "It must be the elder!" Kayla thought.

"My name is Kinoo, short for **Gi**-*kinoo Ah*-**mah**-*gayd*-**nini**, meaning 'He Who Teaches.' I welcome you to the teaching lodge, the *kinoo-maa*-**geg**-*amik* of the Three Fires Midewiwin Lodge. What you just witnessed a moment ago was a good sign. Migizi, the bald eagle, is here with us today for this special teaching. According to our beliefs, migizi must fly over our land and make sure we are following our original instructions and way of life.

"Please," he gestured with his right arm, "I invite you all into our teaching lodge. Find a place to sit and get comfortable. We've got a lot to talk about!"

As Kayla and her best friend, Carly, walked through the open doorway of the lodge, Kayla noticed the familiar scent of burned cedar-tree needles. She remembered that her grandpa's clothes used to smell that way. She had loved that smell! Kayla recalled that her grandfather was very proud of his Ojibwe heritage and wondered if he, too, had come here for ceremonies and teachings when he was alive. She missed her grandpa.

They walked through the lodge toward the fire. The scent of the cedar mingled with the woody smoke coming from the small fire burning in the center of the lodge. The sun cast an angled beam of light down through the square hole in the roof, through the light haze of smoke and onto the grassy lodge floor. Kayla already felt at home here. Her skin tingled! It felt as if her grandfather's spirit *was* there with her!

Kayla and Carly sat down. The other kids from Birch River Elementary School were also entering the lodge and one of the girls sat down next to Kayla.

"Hi, my name is Kayla. It's nice to meet you," said Kayla smiling.

"I'm Raven. It's nice to meet you, too," the girl replied.

Kayla glanced over to where TJ was sitting. "Oh my gosh!" Kayla said to both girls, "TJ's putting grass down the back of that kid's shirt! He's going to get us all into BIG trouble!"

Chapter 2

Sacred Scrolls, Rock Carvings, and a Wampum Belt

Once everyone was seated, Kinoo sat on a wooden bench with a bundle on it and began. "*Boozhoo,* again, everyone," he said, in a softer tone this time. "Please allow me to introduce myself. I am considered to be one of the spiritual leaders of my people, the Anishinabe *(**Ah**-nish-i-**nah**-bay).*" Waving his arm slowly from left to right, Kinoo explained, "The Anishinabe are indigenous (Native) people who live in a vast area stretching from the Atlantic coast of the northeastern United States and eastern Canada, to the west, beyond the Great Lakes. We go by many names, including Mi'kmaq, Odawa, Potawatami, and many others. My people are called the Ojibwe, and they are considered to be

the keepers of the songs and ceremonies. I am also a traditional, hereditary keeper of the Seven Fires Prophecy."

Kinoo reached into the bundle next to him and pulled out a leather bag which he laid on top of the bundle.

"I wonder what's in the bag?" thought Kayla. She glanced over at Raven. Looking straight ahead, Raven wasn't volunteering any hints as to the contents of the bag! "I wonder if *she* knows what's in it?" Kayla pondered.

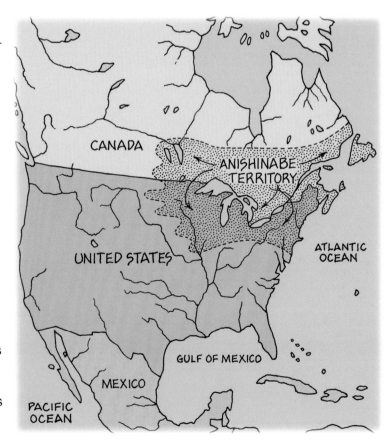

Kinoo continued, "Many indigenous people around the world did not have a written language. They had to remember the history and sacred knowledge of their people and then pass down that knowledge verbally to the next generations. This is called oral tradition.

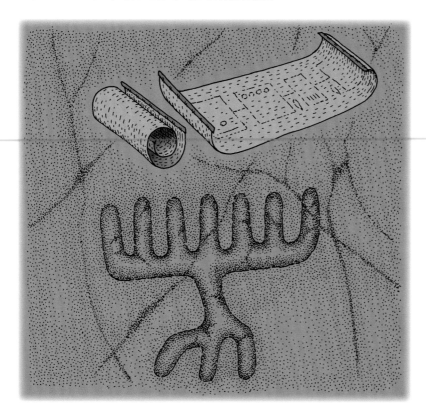

"They created pictures and symbols that served as reminders of this knowledge. For example, the Anishinabe recorded important teachings by writing symbols on birch bark (**wee**-*gwas*) scrolls. They also made rock carvings and drawings. A pictograph of the Seven Fires Prophecy, a gift from prophets given to the Anishinabe people, was carved into rock a very long time ago. Later, several identical wampum belts were also created to record the Seven Fires Prophecy, and we now use one of these belts for special teachings. When I recount the story in the belt, I look at the seven diamonds and I'm reminded of what each prophet said."

Kinoo bent over and untied the top flap of the leather bag. He opened the bag, and ever so carefully he pulled out a long purple and white wampum belt. Kinoo held it up for everyone to see. It was a full six feet long and four inches wide!

Kayla whispered, "Isn't it beautiful? The beads are so smooth and shiny!" Carly and Raven nodded.

Holding the belt horizontally in front of him, using both hands, Kinoo explained the belt. "As you can see, woven into the background of dark purple beads are seven white diamonds. Each diamond represents one of the seven prophecies in the Seven Fires belt. If you look closely you can see that the diamond in the middle is actually two overlapping diamonds.

"This wampum belt is made of shell beads that come from the quahog *(koh-hog)* clam and whelk shells of the Atlantic coastal waters," Kinoo said.

"Now, the prophecy I'm going to tell you about is not a fairy tale," Kinoo continued. "This is a true story given to my people. It is meant to teach us about the future of all people who live on Turtle Island, or as many of you call it, the North American continent.

"It is important to share this story with you at this time, because we are experiencing global climate changes, continued pollution, overuse of our environmental resources, and wars. We must change these things now, before it is too late. I'm asking you to join me in the quest to save our Earth and create peace. The prophecies remind us that we need to take positive action now, in order to balance our minds, our hearts, and Earth."

13

Chapter 3

The Seven Fires Prophecy

Kinoo pointed to the first white diamond on the belt with an eagle feather and began recounting the Seven Fires Prophecy.

"According to our traditional teachings, seven different prophets gave the Seven Fires Prophecy to the Anishinabe people long ago, before the arrival of the Europeans. These prophets could see into the future. They told of events that could come to pass on the North American continent and how they could affect not only those living there, but also the rest of the world. Each of the prophecies was called a fire and each fire referred to a particular period of time that would come in the future. Thus, the teachings of the Seven Prophets are now called the Seven Fires Teaching *(neesh-**wa**-swi ish-ko-**day**-kawn)* of the Anishinabe. This is a special story, even special for all of you, because you will help create the ending!"

❧ The Great Migration ☙

Kinoo pointed to the first three white diamonds with his eagle feather. "The first three prophets *(nee-**gawn**-na-kayg)* told the Anishinabe who lived on the Atlantic coast that they needed to come together and follow the sacred Megis Shell to their chosen land in the West where the wild rice *(man-**o**-min)* grows.

The leadership and ceremonies of the Midewiwin Lodge would give them much spiritual strength on such a journey. They were warned to move or be destroyed. There were many stopping places along the way. Some of the Anishinabe people chose to settle along the migration route and set up permanent villages. Those who continued following the sacred Megis Shell ended the migration at Madeline Island, near the western end of Lake Superior. It took approximately five hundred years for the great migration to take place.

"Not all of the Anishinabe moved west. Some stayed behind and still remain on the northeast coast of Turtle Island. However, as history has shown us, because of the events that followed after the coming of the light-skinned race, many of them died due to wars and foreign diseases. Much of their culture and language was lost, but fortunately, a few remembered the old knowledge and passed it on to the next generations."

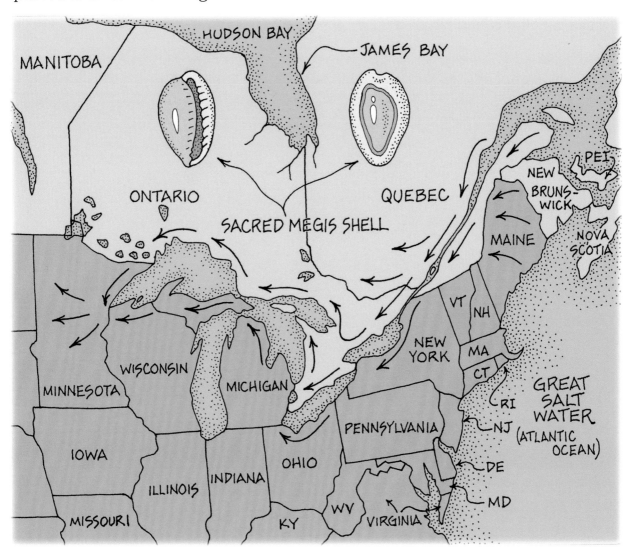

❧ Face of Brotherhood? ❧

Next, Kinoo pointed to the double diamonds on the belt.

"The Fourth Fire was originally given to the Anishinabe by two prophets. These two diamonds represent them. They told of the coming of the light-skinned race.

"One of the prophets said, 'You will know the future of our people by the face the light-skinned race wears. If they come wearing the face of brotherhood *(nee-kon-**nis**-i-win)*, then there will come a time of wonderful change for generations to come. They will bring new knowledge and articles that can be joined with the knowledge of this country. In this way, two nations will join to make a mighty nation. This new nation will be joined by two more, so that four will form the mightiest nation of all. You will know the face of brotherhood if the light-skinned race comes carrying no weapons, if they come bearing only their knowledge and a handshake.'"

◦◦◦ Or Face of Death? ◦◦◦

"The other prophet said, 'Beware if the light-skinned race comes wearing the face of death *(nih-**boo**-win)*. You must be careful because the face of brotherhood and the face of death look very much alike. If they come carrying a weapon . . . beware. If they come in suffering . . . they could fool you. Their hearts may be filled with greed for the riches of this land. You shall know that the face they wear is one of death if the rivers run with poison and the fish become unfit to eat.'"

Kinoo stopped and looked at the children. "Well," he said, "which one do you think we encountered?" Raven, the girl sitting next to Kayla raised her hand.

"Yes?" asked Kinoo.

"I think it was the face of nih-**boo**-win," she said.

"Yes, for the most part, that's what we encountered. We have also seen our rivers poisoned and our fish become unfit to eat," replied Kinoo.

TJ, who had finally decided to listen, raised his hand and said, "But not all of the people of the light-skinned race were bad! What about their children?"

"You're right," said Kinoo. "Not all of the light-skinned race wore the face of death. Maybe there's another message the two prophets have brought us. Does anyone have an idea?"

A boy raised his hand and asked, "Is it that there are two sides to everybody?"

"Yes, very good answer," said Kinoo. "This is what we're going to talk about later on. All people, no matter what race they are, have the choice to make positive decisions or negative decisions."

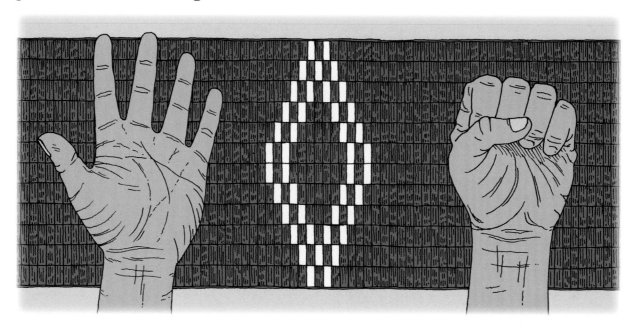

🐚 The Great Struggle of All Native People 🐚

Kinoo continued by pointing to the next diamond.

"The Fifth Prophet said, 'In the time of the Fifth Fire there will come a time of great struggle that will affect the lives of all Native people. During this era, one of great promise will come. If the people accept this new way and abandon the old teachings, then the struggle of the Fifth Fire will be with the people for many generations. This new way will cause the near destruction of the Native people.'

"At the time of these predictions," Kinoo said, "many people scoffed at the prophets. They had medicines *(mush-**kee-ki**-wi-nun)* to keep away sickness. They were healthy and happy people then.

"However, it would not be long before they found that this prophecy would prove true. The light-skinned race launched a military attack on the Native

people throughout the country, aimed at taking away their land and their independence as a free and sovereign people. It is thought that the false promise was the materials and riches embodied in the way of life of the light-skinned people. The prom-ise of this new way of life, through accepting the Eu-ropean culture and beliefs, proved to be very harmful to the Native people. For most, there was no choice, as children were taken from their families and the teachings of the elders, and put into missionary boarding schools.

"Many families were removed from their homelands where traditional foods and other resources for living were abundant. They were taken to small reser-vations on the poorest land. These were big factors in causing the near de-struction of many Native people. They were very quickly being forced to forget their traditional culture. Soon, many of them would become sick, depressed, and lose their will to live.

"In the confusing times of the Sixth Fire, it is said that a group of wise people came among the Anishinabe. They gathered all the spiritual leaders of the Midewiwin Lodge. They told these spiritual leaders that their traditional Midewiwin life was in danger of being destroyed. They gathered all the sacred bundles and the birch bark *(wee-**gwas**)* scrolls that recorded the ceremonies. All these things were placed in a hollowed-out log from the ironwood tree *(mah-**no**-nay)*. Men were lowered over a cliff by long ropes. They dug a hole in the cliff and buried the log where no one could find it.

"Thus the teachings of the elders were hidden out of sight, but not out of memory. It was said that when the time came that the Native people could practice their religion without fear, that a little boy would dream where the ironwood log, full of sacred bundles and scrolls, was buried. He would then lead his people to the place where it had been hidden."

❧ The Seventh Fire: A Time to Re-think Our Ways ❧

"The Seventh Prophet that came to the people was said to be different from the other prophets. He was young and had a mysterious light in his eyes. He said, 'In the time of the Seventh Fire, new people *(osh-ki-bi-**ma**-di-zeeg)* will emerge. They will want to learn the things that were forgotten and will approach the elders to ask them for help in their search. Some of the elders will be ready to teach the new people the ancient traditional knowledge and will be happy to do so. It will be a challenge for the new people to find those elders, but they will find them — if they search carefully and approach them respectfully.

"'If the new people remain strong in their search and listen to the elders, the Waterdrum of the Midewiwin Lodge will again be heard. There will be a rebirth of the Anishinabe Nation and a reawakening of old flames. The sacred fire will again be lit.'

"We recognize that the time of the Seventh Fire has come, as we now hold our ceremonies with our sacred Waterdrum and sacred fire four times a year.

"The prophet of the Seventh Fire cautions the four races of people living on Turtle Island that they need to think and make their choices in a new way. If they make the right choices, then the Seventh Fire will light the Eighth and final Fire, an eternal fire of peace, love, brotherhood, and sisterhood. If they make the wrong choices, they will cause much suffering to all of Earth's people."

Kinoo continued, "Traditional Midewiwin people of the Ojibwe and people from other nations have interpreted the choice to be between the path of technology and the path of spirituality. They feel that in the past two hundred years, many technologies have been developed without wisdom, leading to a modern society that has damaged Earth. Could it be that this unguided approach to technological development represents a rush to destruction? The

path of spirituality and wisdom represents a slower and more thoughtful path that traditional Native people have traveled before and are now seeking again."

Kinoo paused for a moment and looked around the circle, then he continued. "Do you think we can form a new, shared path that includes both ways? Can we build a path together that embraces a more spiritual, thoughtful lifestyle while using technologies that are created using the wisdom of the heart and mind? Do we perhaps need to return to using simpler, more Earth-friendly technologies?"

"This is a time when we need to think with our what?" asked Kinoo.

"Our minds!" shouted the kids.

"Yes, but also, with what else?" asked Kinoo.

"Our hearts!" they said.

"Yes!" said Kinoo. "We need to use both."

Kinoo continued, "Indigenous people all over the world still possess the wisdom of how to think with their minds and hearts. If we bring this way of decision-making into our lives, it will help us create the positive change we need to make. We are living in the time of the Seventh Fire. It's up to all of us to determine if the Seventh Fire will light the Eighth and final Fire of peace and healing. If we make the right choices, we will be successful! Are we the new people of the Seventh Fire? Could you be the Children of the Seventh Fire?"

Chapter 4

What Does It Mean for Us?

Kinoo silently looked around the room. Everyone was quiet, thinking about the prophecy he had just shared with them.

Shiishibens **(Shee**-shih-bens*)*, an Ojibwe boy sitting on the far side of the circle, slowly raised his hand. "Kinoo," he asked, "do you think there is anything I can do during this time of the Seventh Fire to help light the Eighth Fire of healing?"

"Of course," Kinoo replied. "You can do many things. First, when we talk about joining our four races together to form one mighty nation, what comes to your mind?"

"Well," Shiishibens replied, "we can all start being nice to each other, no matter what skin color we have or where we're from. We're all the same on the inside."

"Yes," Kinoo replied, "love, respect, and acceptance of each other is where it will start. From there we can cooperate and learn much from one another. If we listen fully to our hearts and each other, we will come to an agreement about how best to take care of Turtle Island. It takes everyone's effort, especially yours, because you are the ones who this world is being passed on to.

"Do you see the double diamonds in the middle of the belt?" Kinoo asked.

"Yes, and I'm a little confused about what they mean," Shiishibens replied.

"The double diamonds represent the two prophets who came as one. We also know that they represent the forces of right and wrong within each of us.

"It is also said that the double diamonds represent the four races that now live here on Turtle Island. It is our hope that they will live in love, respect, and understanding with each other," Kinoo said. "If we focus on the ways we are similar, like wanting peace and a healthy environment, not the differences, like skin color or religion, we can create harmony. This is an important part of becoming the great and mighty nation spoken of in the prophecy," Kinoo continued.

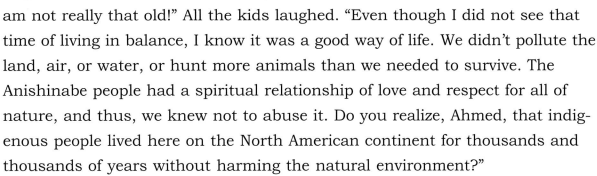

Ahmed raised his hand with a question. "Kinoo, can you tell me a little about what it was like in the time when the natural people lived in balance? It sounded like a nice way to live."

Kinoo replied, "Ahmed, how old do you think I am?! I might look like I may have lived with the dinosaurs, but I am not really that old!" All the kids laughed. "Even though I did not see that time of living in balance, I know it was a good way of life. We didn't pollute the land, air, or water, or hunt more animals than we needed to survive. The Anishinabe people had a spiritual relationship of love and respect for all of nature, and thus, we knew not to abuse it. Do you realize, Ahmed, that indigenous people lived here on the North American continent for thousands and thousands of years without harming the natural environment?"

"Wow, that's a long time," commented Ahmed.

Kinoo continued, "When the colonists arrived, the land, water, and air were pure. Everything living here existed in full health and abundance, including the indigenous people. However, in a short amount of time, the environment has become damaged as a result of modern society. Some of the worst of the environmental damage is through the fossil-fuel-based carbon emissions from automobiles, industry, and power plants into the atmosphere. These are the major causes of global warming, and it's one of our most important environmental problems.

"The best way you can help, Ahmed, is to live a balanced life through the choices you make," said Kinoo. "I have some ideas of simple, practical ways young people can make a difference.

"Recycle tin cans and glass and plastics. Ask your school to buy recycled paper products so we can save our forests," Kinoo began. "By recycling all kinds of materials, we can conserve energy and reduce carbon emissions by up to ninety-five percent in some cases! As a result, we will lessen our need for natural gas, coal, and nuclear energy sources, which are our most polluting and dangerous sources for electricity.

"If we use energy-conserving light bulbs and appliances, and turn them off when they're not needed, we can reduce our energy consumption. Some schools are taking steps to become more energy-efficient. You can suggest to your teachers that your school make energy-conscious decisions, too."

Kinoo continued, "Some families are deciding to create their own electricity by installing solar energy panels. Some states even help pay for these solar energy panels. Through creating your own clean energy you'll feel good about not contributing to pollution.

"Writing to your Governor, State Representatives, Congressmen, and the President to request that they pass tougher laws to protect our environment is another way to create positive change.

"You also can make a difference by becoming a responsible consumer. Ask your parents to buy things that are made by companies who have a good environmental report card and who treat their employees fairly. There are booklets that list these environmentally and socially responsible companies. When you and your parents go shopping, bring one of these booklets with you and use it to buy from the most responsible companies!"

Nathan, who had been waiting patiently for his turn, raised his hand. "Kinoo," he said, "how can we lead more spiritual lives? Is it too late?"

"No Nathan," Kinoo answered, "it's not too late. Leading a more spiritual life involves treating everyone and everything with respect. Be nice to others. Treat others and Earth the way you would want to be treated.

"As well," continued Kinoo, "always give thanks to the Creator for what you have. That's called having gratitude.

"We can also lead more spiritual lives by showing our respect for Earth in
other practical ways. For instance we might try leading simpler lives with fewer

material goods. Reducing how much we buy is a good start. Buying everything we wanted would be greedy, wouldn't it?" Kinoo asked the kids. They didn't answer, but a lot of them were deep in thought.

Kinoo continued, "Buying more stuff means more of our natural resources will be used up. The air and water will become further polluted from the production of these unnecessary things. Happiness cannot be gained from buying more and more things.

"Real happiness comes from within, by being a giving, loving, and respectful human being," Kinoo said with a smile.

Chapter 5

Grow a Garden!

Then Kinoo said, "A great way to reconnect with nature and honor Earth would be to raise your own organic vegetable garden. Or you can buy your vegetables from a local organic farmers market or health food store. Did you know that a lot of the big farms growing the vegetables for your supermarket pollute the land with harmful pesticides, herbicides, and artificial fertilizers? These poisons pollute our water and kill insects, birds, and other wildlife! If you want to buy foods that aren't sprayed with these poisons, look for labels that say ORGANIC on them."

Kinoo stopped and looked around the lodge. He had a little twinkle in his eyes. He asked, "Does anybody here still live and work on a family farm?" All the students from Kayla's class looked at TJ.

TJ refused to raise his hand. Soon, all the kids from Birch River Elementary School were looking at TJ, too!

Kinoo addressed TJ and asked, "Young man, what is your name?"

"Uh, TJ," he said quietly.

"TJ, why don't you come up here and stand next to me," said Kinoo.

TJ shyly shuffled his way up to where Kinoo was standing, not at all knowing what to expect next!

"TJ," Kinoo said, looking at him. "I really admire farmers. They're some of the hardest working people I know. I bet you've learned a lot, working on your parent's farm."

"Yes sir," mumbled TJ, still hanging his head down in a shy manner. You could hardly see TJ's face under the brim of his baseball cap.

"I have an idea," said Kinoo. "How would you like to start an organic vegetable garden at your school? I've already spoken to Mrs. Tomlin, and she thinks it's a great idea."

TJ just stood there for a few seconds, a little shocked at both the compliment about being a farmer and the question about starting a garden!

"Ummm, yeah sure, that sounds cool," said TJ, looking up a bit and trying not to smile. "But, I have a lot of chores at home. I don't know if I have time."

"Okay. No problem," replied Kinoo. "Who from TJ's school would like to help him with the vegetable garden?"

Kayla, Carly, and a few other kids raised their hands.

"Great! TJ, there's your garden crew," said Kinoo. "Put them to good use. Since you already do a lot of physical work on your parents' farm, you can be the planner for this garden project. The garden crew can help you with the work."

Looking out at the circle of kids again, Kinoo rubbed his chin. "Who from the Birch River Elementary School would like to create an organic class garden?" asked Kinoo.

Raven's arm shot up in less than half a second. "I do!" replied Raven excitedly.

"Good! C'mon up here Raven," said Kinoo. "Who will help Raven?" Kinoo asked. Five of her Ojibwe classmates raised their hands.

With one hand on TJ's shoulder and his other on Raven's, Kinoo said to them, "I'm very happy you have both chosen this responsibility. You are leaders in your classes and will set a good example for the others to follow. I will expect to speak with you both in two weeks to review your plans for how you will prepare and plant your gardens. Raven, I know your Aunt Sheri and she has a very green thumb. Maybe you could ask her for some guidance. She can show you how to plant a Three Sisters garden of corn, beans, and squash. If TJ's garden crew is interested, you could travel to Johnston Elementary School to teach them about this Native method of companion planting and explain why it's so successful. This exchange of information is an example of what it means for us to create a shared path together. We exchange ideas and wisdom in how we do things so that it's done in a good, thoughtful way — for us and our Earth."

Raven and TJ both smiled at each other.

the Three Sisters

Chapter 6

Body, Mind, and Spirit

Mylay, who had been waiting patiently with a question, raised her hand and asked, "Kinoo, what did you mean when you talked about the natural people of Earth?"

"Well," Kinoo began, "all societies originally lived in a natural way. It was the way of respect and love for each other and their environment. Learn about your culture's ancient past and you may be surprised to find that they were a lot like mine.

"One way to get back to a natural way of living is to spend some time outside in nature. By spending time outside, you will begin to develop an appreciation and respect for it. What we love and respect, we will care for. Explore your backyard. Create wildlife habitats! Take a hike with friends. Go to the park and discover the beautiful plants, birds, and animals around you. Grow a garden! Reconnecting with nature is an important step to becoming loving caretakers of our Earth.

"One of the last, but very important things to remember during this time of the Seventh Fire is that we need to keep our bodies and minds healthy. That means we cannot abuse drugs, alcohol, or cigarettes. If you don't take care of yourself, how will you be able to take care of Earth and each other?

"As you go out into the world and live your lives, try to follow the Seven Sacred Teachings of the Midewiwin Lodge. They are wisdom, love, respect, bravery, honesty, humility, and truth. These guiding principles will help you make the right decisions during this time of the Seventh Fire. If enough people make the right decisions, it will create the possibility for the Seventh Fire to light the Eighth and final Fire of peace and healing on the planet.

"You have all learned the lesson of the Seven Fires Prophecy well," said Kinoo. "You have started two gardening projects that will benefit your classes, your schools, and your communities. There are so many more wonderful things you can accomplish if you listen to your hearts and listen to each other.

"I'd like to wrap this up with a big thank you *(**chi** mi-**gwetch**)* for coming to hear the teachings of my people. Mrs. Tomlin says she would like to bring you back to hear more of our teachings later this spring. Until then, I wish you well with your garden projects and I'm expecting you to bring me a lunch bag full of my favorite — baby spinach!" said Kinoo, laughing. "Most importantly," he said, "remember that you are Children of the Seventh Fire."

"Thank you, Kinooooo," everyone said.

Then What Did They Do?

KAYLA discovered through talking with **RAVEN** afterwards that they are cousins! Raven invited her to come to the reservation for two weeks that summer to visit her. Raven, Kayla, and several other students, along with Raven's aunt, Sheri, tended the vegetable plants in the Birch River Elementary School garden. Aunt Sheri was very happy Raven had asked her to share her knowledge about this indigenous method of growing corn, beans, and squash. Aunt Sheri also took the girls out into the woods and meadows to help gather wild medicines and traditional foods, like sweet berries! Raven and her aunt drove down to Johnston Elementary School and taught TJ and his class all about the Three Sisters gardening method and why it is beneficial. Kayla was thankful her new auntie and cousin were teaching her about her Ojibwe heritage. She felt peaceful and happy, and looked forward to many more visits. Maybe she would even go with them to the Midewiwin ceremonies, like her grandfather did!

KAYLA and **TJ** had fun working together creating the garden with their classmates. They became great friends again. It was just like the old days, only better! They were finally able to share, once again, their love of nature.

TJ went home and spoke to his parents about the class garden project. They said, yes, he could participate, and they also said that he was excused from some of his chores on the farm! TJ and his classmates busied themselves for the next few weeks, finding out how to create an organic class garden. They received help from the master gardeners at the local cooperative extension office and some of the parents who liked to garden. Over the summer months, he talked with his parents about how they should convert their farm to grow only naturally produced crops. If they started to farm using organic farming practices next spring, they could become a Certified Organic Farm within several years. Oh, by the way, nobody teased TJ any more and he became the nice kid he used to be.

CARLY joined and is now heading up a team of other classmates who are helping with fundraising, finding donations of materials, and creating community support for the class garden.

SHIISHIBENS went home that day and told his parents about the state assistance program to help families afford clean solar power technologies. He and his family are now able to generate their own electricity from solar panels installed on their rooftop. After having the solar panels installed, Shiishibens decided he wanted to become a teacher in the field of renewable energy technologies. He hopes to apply some of the traditional environmental knowledge he is learning from his elders to what he will teach in this growing field of technology.

Shiishibens and his father invited TJ to visit and they went on a hunting trip. Shiishibens' father taught them how to track animals and set traps.

AHMED decided that he wanted to start doing more to promote world peace by erecting a Peace Pole at Johnston Elementary School. He and the students in his class raised the money to buy a Peace Pole from the World Peace Prayer Society and they had a school-wide gathering to promote peace on Earth. The four-sided, 6-foot-tall wooden post reads, "May Peace Prevail on Earth" in four languages.

NATHAN has been very involved with his synagogue and does a lot of volunteer work on Sundays. He visits elderly people in the rest homes around Johnston and brings them lots of smiles and good conversation! He hopes to become a rabbi someday.

MYLAY, on her return home, decided to create wildlife habitats in her backyard. She went onto the National Wildlife Federation Backyard Wildlife Program website and found some easy and fun things to do with her parents, to make their backyard attract more birds and butterflies. It even had directions for making a small pond and garden! Mylay and her family were so inspired by the new wildlife in their backyard that they began planning a trip to a national park the next summer.

Children of the Seventh Fire Pledge

This is an agreement with myself that:

I will do my best to follow the Seven Sacred Teachings which are

Wisdom, Love, Respect, Bravery, Honesty, Humility, and Truth.

I will remember to treat others as I would like to be treated.

When there's a conflict, I will listen to others and

use reason, not physical violence.

I will treat the natural environment with respect.

I will treat all animals with respect.

I will listen to my elders, for they

have wisdom to guide me.

I will honor the gift of my life by

keeping my body, mind, and spirit healthy.

I pledge to make this world a better place to live,

one thought and   one act at a time.

My Name: Today's Date:

_____   _____

Glossary

Account — An explanation, description, or story

Activist — A person who takes positive action to create social or political change

Ancient — Having existed a long time ago

Balance — To bring into harmony

Climate — The average weather conditions of a place as determined by the temperature and meteorological changes over a period of years

Companion planting — A beneficial technique of planting certain types of vegetables next to each other

Conserve — To keep from being wasted

Diminish — To reduce in size, degree, or importance

Financially — Implies reference to money matters, especially where large sums of money are involved

Herbicides — Harmful chemicals used to kill weeds in crop fields, gardens, and lawns

Indigenous — Existing, growing, or produced naturally in a region or country

Interpreted — To explain the meaning of

Megis Shell — Certain members of the Anishinabe had dreams or visions of the Megis Shell showing them which way to travel in their migration westward. This shell also is used ceremonially by the Midewiwin Lodge. More information describing the significance of the Megis Shell can be found in Edward Benton-Banai's *The Mishomis Book*.

Midewiwin Lodge — Consisting of initiated members, this is the original spiritual way and keeper of the sacred knowledge, songs, and ceremonies of and for the Anishinabe people

Organic farming — Growing vegetables without using chemical pesticides or herbicides

Pesticides — Harmful chemicals used to kill insects and other pests on crop fields, flower gardens, and lawns

Philosophy — A particular system of principles for the conduct of life

Pictograph — A picture or picture-like symbol representing an idea, story, or historical events

Prediction — To foretell a future event

Prophecy — A prediction about what events may come to pass in the future

Prophet — Someone who can see into the future

Rebirth — A second birth, or a reawakening

Representing — A symbol that stands for an object, person, or place

Seven Fires Prophecy — The teachings of the Seven Prophets

Sincere — Truthful, straightforward, honest

Sovereign — Independent of all others

Spiritual — Sacred, devotional, not lay or temporal

Traditional — Pertaining to or in agreement with a long established custom or practice

Translated — Has been, or to have been, put into the words of a different language

Turtle Island — The Anishinabe name for the North American continent

Waterdrum — The sacred drum of the Midewiwin Lodge, a very important object used in the lodge ceremonies. The term holds much meaning, more than can be explained here. For a more detailed explanation, see Edward Benton-Banai's *The Mishomis Book*.

Resources

(**K** = for Kids; **P** = for Parents; **T** = for Teachers)

Story-Related Fun and Educational Materials for Kids, Parents, and Teachers

Books

A Teacher's Activity and Skills Guidebook for Children of the Seventh Fire by Lisa Hart, 2011. Shokan, NY: Big Oak Press. **T, P**

How to Grow a School Garden — A Complete Guide for Parents and Teachers by Arden Bucklin-Sporer and Rachael Kathleen Pringle, 2010. Portland, OR: Timber Press. **P, T**

The Mishomis Book: The Voice of the Ojibway by Edward Benton-Banai, 1988. Hayward, WI: Indian Country Communications. **K, P, T**

Better World Shopping Guide by Ellis Jones, 2006. Gabriola Island, BC: New Society Publishers. **K, P, T**

Web Sites

Children of the Seventh Fire — Shows what other kids are doing in their communities to protect and restore the environment and create peace! *www.childrenoftheseventhfire.com* **K, P, T**

Three Sisters Garden — Provides instructions for planting a Three Sisters garden. *www.kidsgardening.com/growingideas/projects/march02/mar02-pg1.htm* **P, T**

Solar Power Rocks — Lists solar power incentives. *www.solarpowerrocks.com* **P, T**

Morning Earth — Features nature-based visual art, dance, and poetry; famous naturalists; and artist Andrew Goldsworthy. *www.morning-earth.org* **K, P, T**

Care2 KIDS ONLY! — Has many great links to other kid-friendly web sites about nature. *www.care2.com/channels/ecoinfo/kids* **K, P, T**

Kids For Saving Earth — Provides an environmental education curriculum for all ages. *www.kidsforsavingearth.org* **K, P, T**

Hudson River Sloop Clearwater — An award winning environmental education organization founded by Pete Seeger. *www.clearwater.org* **K, P, T**

Project Learning Tree, Project Wild!, and Project WET — Environmental education for educators and students, grade levels Pre-k through 12. *www.plt.org, www.projectwild.org, www.projectwet.org* **T, P**

National Wildlife Federation — Offers fun ways to get kids to experience nature for one hour every day! *www.greenhour.org* **P**

Tom Brown Jr.'s Tracking, Awareness and Survival Education School — Offers outdoor workshops for nature-based living. *www.trackerschool.com* **P, T**

North American Integrative Indigenous Knowledge-based Programs

Web Sites

Institute for Integrative Science and Health — Brings together indigenous ways of knowing and Western scientific knowledge. Cheryl Bartlett, Director. *www.integrativescience.ca* **P, T**

University of Minnesota: An Ojibwe Arts in Education Model Program — Combines Ojibwe arts and culture with a standards-based curriculum. *www.intersectingart.umn.edu* **P, T**

Alaska Native Knowledge Network: Handbook for Culturally Responsive Science Curriculum — Presents a culturally relevant curriculum that integrates indigenous and Western knowledge in science. *www.ankn.uaf.edu/publications/handbook* **P, T**

Source for Educational Empowerment and Community Development (SEED) — Offers conferences, classes, and workshops to facilitate bridging indigenous wisdom and modern knowledge. *www.seedgraduateinstitute.org* **P, T**

Dr. Leroy Little Bear — Promotes the exploration and discussion of the importance of indigenous perspective in today's scientific thought. Email: *littlebear@uleth.ca* **P, T**

Classroom Resources

Web Sites

Children of the Seventh Fire — Lots of great educational resources for kids! Students can send in a description of their projects (with photos!) to be posted on this web site — *www.childrenoftheseventhfire.com.* The author's **Classroom Visiting Program** can be arranged through this web site and orders can be placed for her book *A Teacher's Activity and Skills Guidebook for Children of the Seventh Fire.* **P, T**

Three Fires Midewiwin Lodge — For further information visit *http://www.three-fires.net/tfn/index.htm* or contact *www.rgaywish@mymts.net* **K, P, T**

Native Tech — Provides extensive educational information about Native American Technology and Art. *www.NativeTech.org* **K, P, T**

World Peace Prayer Society — Includes information about Peace Pole projects and the International Peace Pals program. *www.worldpeace.org* **K, P, T**

THIS BOOK IS DEDICATED TO ALBERT R. PUDVAN

FOREWORD

Ever wonder when you see a city on a map, "Why here?" Sometimes the answer is obvious. A conspiracy of geography and economics. Royal edict. Natural resources. All these are good reasons to start a city, but what keeps it growing and alive?

Part of the answer may lie in what Chicago has become. Proud, young, aggressive, reaching, daring, experimenting, redefining and remaking itself again and again. Attractive qualities that draw and keep people here.

Cities are like fountains. Fountains exist only so long as water flows through them. They change their temperament with the subtleties of the water. Cut off the water and they become inert statues of stone. Cities exist as long as people live in them. If there is nothing to pull people here and give them hope - the city, too, becomes nothing more than stone. Give people free reign of energy and expression, and the city surges upward without bound.

Even the buildings testify to that. The Sears Tower, which is visible from every corner of the city and beyond, is itself a city in miniature. It defies gravity hurling millions of tons of steel 1454 feet into the restless Midwest skies. Seventy-eight football fields of floor space are woven together with 43,000 miles of telephone cable, providing workspace for 11,000 people. Biggest, most, largest, best... Chicagoans wouldn't have their showpiece any other way.

Ask them. Ask each and every person in Chicago. You may get 4 million answers but they will have a number of things in common. Their direction is pointed to by the Sears Tower - Their limits are its infinite horizon.

That's why they are here. Over the years a limitless, flowing spirit has grown here. It's not because of a caprice of weather or an accident of history. When that spirit arrived, Chicago had to grow here.

Jay Flynn

A LONG
LONG TIME AGO

Produced, Photographed and Published by: David J. Maenza

Written by: Jay Flynn

Designed by: James Groll

Art Direction by: Paul Collins

Edited by: Bob Hale and Jeanette Rawley

Post Production: Gamma Photo Company

Production Assistance by: Christine Groll

Photo Editor and Manager: Joanne Filippi

Assistant Photo Editor and Designer: Sydney Groll

Contributing Photographers: Francois Paris, Vic Bider, Tony Cimino

Travel and Technical Adviser: Rose Scandura

Associate Editor: Darlene Ficke

Entertainment and Restaurant Adviser: Marina Christiansen

Food Photography by: Michael Comacho

BLACK AND WHITE PHOTOGRAPHY COURTESY OF THE SPECIAL COLLECTION DEPARTMENT, CHICAGO PUBLIC LIBRARY,
AND THE DAVID R. PHILLIPS ARCHIVES

djmpub@cbipc.com

CHICAGO WAS INCORPORATED

AS A TOWN ON AUGUST 12, 1833

WITH A POPULATION OF 350.

WHEN THIS PHOTOGRAPH WAS

TAKEN, THE CITY WAS JUST 55

YEARS OLD.

CITIES ARE LIVING THINGS.
CHICAGO'S BIRTH HIDES IN
LEGEND AND DIM HISTORY. LIKE
MANY CITIES IT TOOK ITS FIRST
HALTING STEPS, FALTERED AND
PICKED ITSELF UP AGAIN. CHICAGO
HAD AN UNRULY ADOLESCENCE
AND THEN IT DIED. FEW LIVING
THINGS RISE AGAIN, ESPECIALLY
WHEN STRUCK DOWN SO YOUNG.
CHICAGO DID. NOT CONTENT
TO REMAIN FORGOTTEN IN THE
PAST, CHICAGO WORKED TO
FULFILL A SEEMINGLY IMPOSSIBLE
FUTURE VISION.

WRIGLEY BUILDING AND MICHIGAN AVENUE BRIDGE, 1900

"BACK IN THE 1920'S, MY LATE FATHER USED
TO COMPETE AGAINST JOHNNY WEISSMULLER IN
CHICAGO RIVER MARATHON SWIMS."

NORMAN ROSS
RADIO PERSONALITY

CITY NEIGHBORHOOD, 1865

The first people to settle along the green shores

of the glacier-carved lake were the Illinois native

Americans. Their name for the place near the

mouth of a slow river was Chicaugou. The name

encompasses nothing of the city's future

greatness. It means "wild onions" which grew

along the marshy shoreline.

EUROPEANS FIRST HEARD OF CHICAGO FROM EXPLORERS AND MISSIONARIES LIKE JOLIET AND MARQUETTE. FORT DEARBORN WAS ESTABLISHED AT WHAT IS NOW THE CORNER OF MICHIGAN AVENUE AND WACKER DRIVE. THE FIRST PERMANENT EUROPEAN SETTLER WAS JEAN BAPTISTE POINT DU SABLE, A MAN OF FRANCO-AFRICAN DESCENT. DU SABLE CAME TO CHICAGO BECAUSE IT STOOD AT THE HEAD OF THE MAIN TRAILS TO THE UNSETTLED WEST. PROPHETICALLY, HE CAME HERE TO TRADE.

CULTURE COMES TO THE "HOG BUTCHER TO THE WORLD" -- THE ART INSTITUTE CA. 1920

THE REBORN CITY GROWS: TURN-OF-THE-CENTURY PARADE ON SOUTH MICHIGAN AVENUE

Through the early and middle 1800's the city boomed. Grain flowed out on newly built railroads. Irish, Poles, Germans, fleeing starvation and tyranny in Europe, and newly-freed African-American slaves flooded the town and Chicago sprawled into a city. Then one searing October night in 1871, the city died.

Michigan Avenue south from Chicago Avenue

Planners like Burnham and Sullivan saw an opportunity to replace disease-plagued sprawl with a model city. URBS IN HORTO, A CITY IN A GARDEN became the motto of the reborn Chicago. Its centerpiece was to be the lake shore, not acres of stone.

The lake shore was given over to almost 25 miles of park and recreation land, Chicago's Front Yard. Inside the city itself, 560 parks testified to the motto.

State Street becomes "that Great Street", 1900

DARING ARCHITECTURE TOOK
ROOT AND STRETCHED TO THE
SKY. CHICAGO IS THE
BIRTHPLACE OF THE FIRST
SKYSCRAPER AND FIRST
ELEVATED TRAIN LINE. TODAY,
THE WORKS OF SULLIVAN,
BURNHAM AND WRIGHT STAND
BESIDE THOSE OF MODERN
ARCHITECTS. MIES VAN DER
ROHE MADE CHICAGO A
PROVING GROUND OF GLEAMING
DREAMS IN STEEL AND GLASS.

SEARS TOWER STANDS AS A MILESTONE TO THE MODERN ERA OF CHICAGO. STILL THE TALLEST BUILDING IN THE WORLD IN

TWO OFFICIAL CATEGORIES, SEARS TOWER STRETCHES FROM THE PRIMEVAL LIMESTONE TO THE CLOUDS. IN ITS SUPERLATIVES

IT REPRESENTS LEAPS OVER COUNTLESS STRUCTURAL OBSTACLES THAT DAUNTED THOSE WITH SMALLER VISIONS.

TOPPING THIS ARCHITECTURAL GIANT IS SEARS TOWER SKYDECK -- "CHICAGO'S HIGHEST ATTRACTION". AT 1,353 FEET

ABOVE THE GROUND, THIS WORLD-CLASS OBSERVATORY OFFERS STUNNING VIEWS COVERING ALL OF CHICAGO AND FOUR

STATES. HIGH SPEED ELEVATORS WHISK GUESTS 103 STORIES SKYWARD IN JUST 70 SECONDS TO

WHERE FLOOR TO CEILING WINDOWS OFFER UNOBSTRUCTED VIEWS IN ALL DIRECTIONS. SINCE ITS

OPENING ON JUNE 22, 1974, SEARS TOWER SKYDECK HAS WELCOMED MORE THAN 30

MILLION GUESTS FROM AROUND THE WORLD.

SEARS TOWER LOOMS 1,450 FEET ABOVE STREET
LEVEL. ON A CLEAR DAY, PARTS OF ILLINOIS,
MICHIGAN, INDIANA AND WISCONSIN CAN BE
SEEN FROM THE SKYDECK.

Chicago is a living museum of architecture. Walking tours criss-cross the city, showing visitors experiments and achievements of both the past and present as cranes nurse new construction skyward.

CHICAGOANS OFTEN PLAY A
GAME OF GUESSING WHAT A NEW
BUILDING WILL LOOK LIKE. A
CASTLE, A GEOMETRIC SPIRE OR
EVEN A WEDDING CAKE ARE SOME
OF THE SUGGESTIONS AS A NEW
IRON GRIDWORK TAKES SHAPE.
AS THE CITY GROWS, IT IS HARD
TO IMAGINE THAT IT WAS
NOTHING BUT ASHES ABOUT 130
YEARS AGO.

"HAVING TRAVELED ALL OVER THE WORLD, I KNOW OF NO OTHER CITY THAT TAKES
AS MUCH PRIDE IN ITSELF AS CHICAGO. THE VITALITY AND TALENT OF THE PEOPLE...
AND THE ENERGY, THE BEAUTY OF THIS CITY, JUST EXCITE ME. AND THE CLIMATE...
WELL, IT MAKES YOU STRONG."

BILL KURTIS,
AWARD-WINNING BROADCAST JOURNALIST

THE TREASURES OF THE PAST ARE FONDLY REVERED AS NEW BUILDINGS ARE AWAITED. THE HISTORIC WATER TOWER, BUILT IN 1869, BEST SYMBOLIZES WHAT THE CITY IS ABOUT. IT WAS PART OF THE DRIVE TO MODERNIZE THE BOOMING FRONTIER TOWN AND IT SURVIVED THE GREAT FIRE, GIVING THE PEOPLE HOPE TO REBUILD. TODAY IT STANDS AT THE HEAD OF THE MAGNIFICENT MILE ON MICHIGAN AVENUE.

Marking the south end of the Magnificent Mile is the Wrigley

Building. Named for the chewing gum magnate, it was built in

stages and finished in 1924. The limestone and terra cotta

facade forms a gleaming backdrop to events on the Chicago

river and the riverwalk, where people can stroll through a

ribbon of parkland all the way to the lakefront.

Wrigley Building

LIKE MOST HOMEOWNERS, CHICAGO KEEPS ITS FRONT YARD TIDY AND MAKES IT A SHOWCASE FOR THE CITY.

THE NECESSITIES OF WAR HAVE CREATED AND RECREATED NAVY PIER. HOWEVER, THE CITY WAS NOT

CONTENT TO ALLOW THE MILE-LONG BUILDING TO LANGUISH INTO DUST.

YEARS OF RECONSTRUCTION HAVE CREATED A FAMILY-FRIENDLY AMUSEMENT AND ENTERTAINMENT CENTER AT NAVY PIER. A SHORT RIDE FROM THE HEART OF THE CITY, IT OFFERS RESTAURANTS, DINNER LAKE CRUISES, RIDES AND CONCERTS.

THE REVITALIZED NAVY PIER BECOMES A WINTER PLAYGROUND

CHICAGO OFFERS CUISINE FROM EVERY CONTINENT TO SUIT EVERY TASTE.

IT'S NOT OFTEN WE GET TO SAIL RIGHT INTO THE HEART OF A CITY. I HAD DECIDED TO MAKE A SAILING TOUR OF THE GREAT LAKES AND WANTED TO BE IN CHICAGO FOR THE START OF THE MACKINAC RACE. OVER THE YEARS, I HAVE DRIVEN OR FLOWN TO CHICAGO, BUT NOTHING MATCHES THE SENSATION OF SAILING RIGHT UP TO THE FOOT OF THE FLASHING BEACONS OF THE SEARS TOWER. AS I CAME DOWN FROM THE NORTH, I COULD SEE THE TOP OF THE SEARS TOWER EVEN BEFORE WE CROSSED THE STATE LINE.

SEVEN-HUNDRED FIFTEEN EAST GRAND AVENUE

AFTER WE BERTHED IN MONROE STREET HARBOR, WE HEADED OVER TO NAVY PIER WHERE MANY OF THE RACING CAPTAINS AND CREWS WERE BEING FETED AT RIVA RESTAURANT (312-644-7482). WE FOUND THE ATMOSPHERE THAT OF AN UPSCALE COASTAL SEAFOOD RESTAURANT. IN BRASS AND MAHOGANY DECOR, WE MET FRESH WATER AND OCEAN SAILORS FROM ALL POINTS OF THE COMPASS ENJOYING A HUGE SELECTION OF LOBSTER AND STEAK DISHES SOME OF THE PARTIES WERE ALSO IN PRIVATE DINING ROOMS.

WE COULD WATCH OUR MEALS BEING PREPARED IN THEIR LARGE EXHIBITION KITCHEN, UNDERNEATH A HUGE

MURAL SHOWING THE HISTORY OF NAVY PIER. OVER DINNER, WE NEVER LOST SIGHT OF THE LAKE, BEING

ENJOYED BY PLEASURE CRAFT OF ALL SIZES. IN THE TWILIGHT, THE VIEW OF THE LAKEFRONT, CHICAGO'S FRONT

YARD WAS AWESOME. WE WERE DOUBLY LUCKY TO BE HERE ON A WEDNESDAY EVENING BECAUSE NAVY PIER

PUTS ON A SPECTACULAR FIREWORKS SHOW.

THE FOOD LIVED UP TO ITS REPUTATION. I HAD THE LINGUINI SCAMPI

DIAVALO, A ZESTY DISH THAT LIVES UP TO ITS DEVILISH NAME - SCAMPI

SAUTEED WITH GARLIC, OLIVE OIL AND CRUSHED RED PEPPERS, SERVED WITH

MARINARA AND A TOUCH OF CREAM. MY FIRST MATE LOVED THE FILET

MIGNON OF TUNA, A MARINATED AND GRILLED TUNA FILET, OFFERED ON A

BED OF HORSERADISH MASHED POTATOES WITH A ROASTED SHALLOT

SAUCE AND PICKLED GINGER. ONE FAMOUS PATRON, WHO JUST HAPPENS TO HAVE BEEN PRESIDENT OF THE

UNITED STATES, ONCE SAID, "IF I KNEW LUNCH WOULD BE THIS GOOD, I WOULD HAVE SKIPPED BREAKFAST."

AFTER DINNER WE SWAPPED SEA TALES UNDER CEILING FANS AT THE FULL BAR AS THE MOON ROSE OVER THE

LAKE. SOME OF THESE MEN AND WOMEN SAILORS HAD BRAVED THE

CHALLENGES OF RIVERS, SEAS AND LAKES ALL OVER THE WORLD. IN OUR

PART OF THE RIVA RESTAURANT THERE MUST HAVE BEEN HUNDREDS OF

YEARS OF EXPERIENCE. WE KNEW LAKE MICHIGAN WOULD TEST THEIR

KNOWLEDGE IN THE COMING DAYS.

LARRY AND SANDRA KING,
DAIRY FARMERS, GREEN BAY, WISCONSIN

OLDER NEIGHBORHOODS, ONCE
THE BASTIONS OF IMMIGRANTS,
DOT THE CITY. FOR ITS
INHABITANTS, CHICAGO IS A
CITY OF NEIGHBORHOODS. EACH
NEIGHBORHOOD HAS ITS OWN
ETHNIC PARADES AND FESTIVALS.
ST. PATRICK'S DAY FINDS THE
RIVER DYED GREEN AND THE
MAYOR LEADING THE PARADE
THROUGH THE CENTER OF THE
CITY. THE SNAP OF FIRE
CRACKERS GREETS CHINESE NEW
YEAR IN CHINATOWN NEAR
WENTWORTH AND CERMAK.
CINCO DE MAYO, POLISH
CONSTITUTION DAY,
OKTOBERFEST, BUD BILLIKEN
DAY, FESTA ITALIANA THE LIST
IS ENDLESS.

A BUSY MAYOR LEADS ONE OF MANY ETHNIC PARADES.

SOMETIMES I FIND MYSELF FLYING HOME AFTER SOME MEETING OR CONVENTION,

REALIZING I HAVEN'T SEEN ANYTHING OF THE CITY I WAS IN EXCEPT THE FOUR

WINDOWLESS WALLS OF THE MEETING ROOM OR CONVENTION HALL. NOT FROM

CHICAGO. I WAS LUCKY ENOUGH TO ATTEND A RECEPTION AT THE CRYSTAL

GARDEN ON NAVY PIER.

THE CRYSTAL GARDEN TAKES FULL ADVANTAGE OF ITS PRIME LOCATION BY

BATHING ITS GUESTS WITH MAJESTIC VIEWS OF THE CITY THROUGH ITS 50-FOOT

ATRIUM WINDOWS. FROM ALMOST A MILE OUT IN THE LAKE, WE COULD SEE A VISTA

THAT SHIFTED FROM SAIL BOATS PLYING EMERALD WATERS AT SUNSET TO THE

SKYLINE DOMINATED BY THE SEARS TOWER SPARKLING UNDER THE STARS.

CALLING IT A GARDEN IS A BIT OF AN UNDERSTATEMENT. WE CHATTED AND

DANCED ALL OVER THIS YEAR-ROUND, INDOOR EDEN. PALM TREES AND LEAP

FROG FOUNTAINS, SPREAD OVER ONE ACRE, MAKE THE CRYSTAL GARDEN A REAL

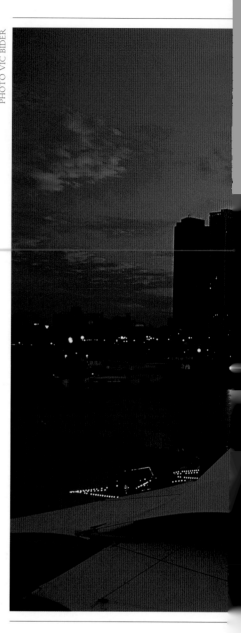

DELIGHT FOR ANY KIND OF RECEPTION

OR CORPORATE EVENT.

OUTSIDE AND ONLY STEPS AWAY ARE THE GIANT FERRIS WHEEL

AND BOAT RIDES ON THE LAKE AND RIVER. THE WAVE RUNNER

BAR AND GRILL AND THE NAVY PIER BEER GARDEN DREW LOTS OF

PEOPLE, SURROUNDING US WITH A CARNIVAL ATMOSPHERE. IMAGINE

HOLDING YOUR NEXT MEETING AT THE CENTER OF ALL THIS, A FEW BLOCKS FROM THE LOOP.

THAT REMINDS ME, I'VE GOT TO CALL (312) 595-5446 AND ORGANIZE A SIT-DOWN DINNER FOR 750

FOR MY FRATERNITY'S NATIONAL CONVENTION.

SYDNEY WINTERHAGEN,
COMMODITY BROKER, NEW YORK CITY

I arrived in Chicago for two weeks of medical lectures, but was delighted to discover that I had plenty of time to enjoy the city. First stop was the Sears Skydeck. As I looked over the stunning view of this fabulous city laid out at my feet, I planned a culinary tour to enjoy the evenings, after full days of conferences and workshops.

The Tavern on Rush satisfied me wonderfully with a huge steak. The more eclectic eateries on Rush Street educated my taste buds. However, I love lasagna and sought out Papa Milano's at the corner of Oak and State. Three colleagues and I were glad to find a quiet, comfortable booth, where we enjoyed cheese lasagna, baked chicken Milano with peas, mushrooms and onions. One of the ladies feasted on a thin-crust pizza while I decided on a rosemary salad and veal Florentine with the fourth-generation Sicilian sauce. We enjoyed wine and cannolis while chatting with the Papa Milano family. They suggested a short stroll to the lake. We enjoyed the warm evening's view of the city from Oak Street Beach.

My only regret was not being able to sample more of the extensive menu. That was short-lived, however. Two days later, we found ourselves behind schedule so I suggested a working lunch. We called 312-787-3710 and had Papa Milano deliver a wonderful midday meal of linguini with calamari sauce, eggplant Parmesan, pasta Fagiol, baked clams and their famous meat lasagna. I will find an excuse to visit Chicago again, but who needs one?

Dr. Wolfgang Kramer
Disseldorf, Germany

Visitors also find the Chicago spirit is contagious and far-reaching. Businesses around the world are eager to share in it. Name a business or field and it probably has its convention in Chicago. Travel, sports, consumer electronics, medicine, film, autos, boats, dogs, cats, antiques are all reasons why Chicago greets more people than already live here as business visitors each year.

THE CROWN OF LIGHT AT THE TOP OF THE JOHN HANCOCK BUILDING CAN BE SEEN FROM THREE STATES.

THE MAGNIFICENT MILE.
CHICAGO'S PREMIER REAL
ESTATE BECOMES A GLITTERING
ORNAMENT FOR THE WINTER
HOLIDAYS. THE DISPLAY OF
LIGHT STRETCHES FROM THE
RIVER TO LAKE SHORE DRIVE.
A BUSINESS AND HOTEL
DISTRICT, NORTH MICHIGAN
AVENUE ALSO BOASTS PREMIER
STORES FROM AROUND THE
WORLD.

I was staying in Chicago for a series of business meetings and wanted a quick break. I decided to save my energy from my heavy schedule and stuck close to my hotel, the Drake on Michigan Avenue.

I am a fanatic about impressionist art and desperately wanted to get down to the Art Institute. Fortunately, I found a very impressive collection right below me.

Galleries Maurice Sternberg (312-642-1700) is right in the Drake Hotel Arcade on the Magnificent Mile. Only a few steps inside, I forgot about my meetings and was being led through the world of 19th and 20th Century American and European Art by the capable Judith Sternberg. The gallery has been a family business for 55 years and all that experience has been passed to Mrs. Sternberg.

She told me how Chicago had become a center of French Impressionist works when the Palmer family assembled a staggering collection of paintings, most of which are now in the Art Institute. In Galleries Sternberg, I could actually contemplate acquiring a masterwork. Mrs.

ONE FORTY EAST WALTON PLACE AT MICHIGAN AVENUE

Sternberg shepherded me through the paintings of Edouard Cortes, Henri Martin and Henri Le Sidaner. Some of these works have been invited to European museum exhibitions. She told me about American painters John George Brown, Hayley Lever and Alexander Calder.

Mrs. Sternberg impressed me not only with her knowledge of art, but her way of learning

about a client. She was helping me find a painting that would suit my tastes and lifestyle and

was willing to take the time to do it.

I left knowing I'd be back. I had seen a work that would be an important addition to my

collection.

Jay Turner,
Art Collector, Park Ridge, Illinois

WINTER CAN MEAN COLD, WIND AND GLOOM. BUT TO CHICAGOANS! IT MEANS HOT CHOCOLATE, ICE SKATING, TOBOGGANING AND CROSS-COUNTRY SKIING. FUN IN THE SNOW AT ALMOST ANY CITY PARK GIVES YOU PLENTY OF EXCUSES TO GET OUTDOORS TO TRY TO CATCH SNOWFLAKES ON YOUR TONGUE.

THE EMERALD CITY: CHICAGO IN WINTER FROM LINCOLN PARK LAGOON

SIX OF US RODE A HORSE-DRAWN CARRIAGE THROUGH THE

AREA KNOWN AS RIVER NORTH.   AFTER DINING AT LINO'S,

WE WANTED TO FINISH THE NIGHT OFF IN RELAXED STYLE

AND HEADED TO THE REDHEAD PIANO BAR JUST WEST OF

STATE STREET AT 16 W. ONTARIO. WE HAD SPOTTED THE

"REDHEAD" SIGN FROM THE SEARS TOWER SKYDECK EARLIER IN THE EVENING. JUST INSIDE, WE EASED PAST THE

BUSY PIANO BAR INTO THE INTIMATE ATMOSPHERE. WALLS LINED WITH SHEET MUSIC AND PHOTOS OF MOVIE

GREATS REVERBERATED FROM THE VARIOUS STANDARD AND POP HITS BEING PLAYED. THE CLIENTELE WAS

WELL-DRESSED AND THE MUSIC UPBEAT. WE HAD A BALL, SINGING ALONG IN CHICAGO'S PREMIER PIANO BAR,

'TIL THE WEE HOURS OF THE MORNING.   A FEW WEEKS LATER WE CALLED (312)

640-1000 TO FIND OUT WHO WAS PLAYING. THIS TIME WE STARTED THE

EVENING AT 8 O'CLOCK WITH COCKTAILS AND MUSIC AT THE REDHEAD. WHAT

A GREAT MUSICAL EVENING!

JON VANDERPELLAN AND FRIENDS,
LA GRANGE, ILLINOIS.

SIXTEEN WEST ONTARIO STREET

All summer long, the Petrillo Band Shell in Grant Park echoes, thunders and dances to music

of every taste. You can sit under the stars and let the notes flow like a cool lake breeze.

Everyone comes down to the Lakefront and celebrates the Fourth of July with fireworks, food

and, of course, jazz.

"When I leave this city, when I
leave this earth, the one thing
I'll know is this: I lived in a city
that truly loved me, and I've
loved them."

Michael Jordan

"CLOSE YOUR EYES AND FEEL THE CITY."

LORI POPPA
ACCOUNTANT
CHICAGO

"CHICAGO WANTS YOU HERE. THEY WANT YOU TO COME. THEY HAVE SO
MANY EASY WAYS INTO THE CITY. THERE ARE NO WALLS, JUST THE LIGHTS TO
GUIDE YOU INTO ITS HEART."

FRANKLIN FEINBERG
INVESTOR
TEL AVIV, ISRAEL

"EVERYTHING IS SO WELL PLANNED AND LAID OUT. IT IS SO CONVENIENT. ALL
THE PLANNING OF THE LAST CENTURY HAS MADE A DIFFERENCE."

ERIKA EDDIE
PROPERTY MANAGER
LUCERNE, SWITZERLAND

OUR DAUGHTER WAS ALWAYS GOOD WITH NUMBERS, SO IT CAME AS NO SURPRISE WHEN SHE TOLD US SHE WANTED TO MAJOR IN ACCOUNTING. HER CHOICE OF SCHOOLING DID SURPRISE US --- UNIVERSITY OF ILLINOIS AT CHICAGO. HOWEVER, WE WERE CONVINCED WHEN SHE TOLD US HOW HIGHLY REGARDED THE SCHOOL WAS. IT STANDS IN THE SHADOW OF THE SEARS TOWER, A VERTICAL CITY AT THE CENTER OF CHICAGO.

SINCE CHARLOTTE HAS STARTED SCHOOL WE HAVE MADE SEVERAL TRIPS TO VISIT HER. RIGHT ON THE EDGE OF CHICAGO'S "LITTLE ITALY" IS ONE OF ITS HIDDEN TREASURES. TAYLOR STREET IS HOME TO MANY RESTAURANTS. TUSCANY, OUR FAVORITE, OFFERS A REAL FAMILY ATMOSPHERE WHICH IS PERFECT FOR US TO PLAY CATCH UP. WE ALSO MEET SOME GREAT LOCALS, LIKE IVO COZZINI, WHO LOVE TO SHARE STORIES ABOUT THE CITY, INCLUDING THE HISTORY OF THE NEIGHBORHOOD.

TEN FOURTEEN WEST TAYLOR STREET

THEY WILL SERVE YOUR FOOD ANY WAY—THEY JUST WANT YOU TO LIKE IT. I HAVE SEEN THE WAITER CAREFULLY GOING OVER THE MENU WITH A NEW PATRON - TO FIND JUST WHAT THEY WOULD ENJOY. BECAUSE THE THREE OF US HAVE SUCH DIFFERENT TASTES, OUR WAITER SUGGESTED AN "ITALIAN SAMPLER" OF VITELLA ALL' ARETINA (SAUTEED MEDALLION OF VEAL WITH SUN-DREID TOMATOES, GOAT CHEESE AND PESTO), SCAMPI AI FERRI (MARINATED GRILLED SCAMPI) AND PETTI DI POLLO AL PALIO (GRILLED BREAST OF CHICKEN WITH FRESH TOMATOES, MOZZARELLA, OLIVE OIL AND BASIL). ALL FINISHED OFF WITH LEMON MANDARINO FOR DESSERT, WE NOW CALL TUSCANY OUR "SECOND HOME".

MRS. JOSEPH HAMMS,
INSURANCE AGENT, DANVILLE, ILLINOIS

"I LOVE PHOTOGRAPHING THE CITY AT NIGHT. IT IS LIKE OPENING A CHEST HEAPED WITH TREASURE. DAZZLING!"

DAVID MAENZA

STATE STREET STORES TRY TO OUT-DECORATE
EACH OTHER AT CHRISTMAS

TEN THIRTY-ONE NORTH RUSH STREET

WE ARE NEW TO CHICAGO. WHEN WE HEARD NORWAY WAS PLAYING JAPAN IN WOMEN'S SOCCER AT

SOLDIER FIELD, MY DAUGHTER WHO GOES TO NORTHWESTERN UNIVERSITY WANTED TO MAKE A BIG DAY

AROUND THIS EVENT. A FRIEND SUGGESTED A PLACE WE HAD NOT HEARD OF BEFORE.

After the game we went to Tavern on Rush. An interesting name! The name is not fancy, just plain and to the point. But Tavern is very modern and classy. And the food delicious!

Marty, one of the owners, showed us to our table where I had a New York Strip Steak (in Chicago, HA!) with the biggest baked potato I had ever seen. My daughter enjoyed the shrimp Ciprioni (homemade square noodles in a cognac cream sauce with jumbo shrimp) and my wife dove into some Ahi Tuna. Our friends celebrated over filet Mignon and baby back ribs.

After dinner we moved to an outdoor table to relax and people watch. We watched the city come to life over cappuccino. There was so much happening. Scottie Pippin, the basketball player, stopped in and boy, is he big!

We know we will like it here in Chicago. There is so much excitement.

Tor Hagmo, Import/Exporter, Bergen Norway
(now Lake Shore Drive, Chicago)

"Hog Butcher for the World
Toolmaker, Stacker of Wheat,
Player with Railroads and the
Nation's Freight Handler;
Stormy, husky, brawling
City of the Big Shoulders:..."

Carl Sanburg
Poet

The early days of the National
Football League: The Chicago Bears
played at Wrigley Field.

North Michigan Avenue: Modern
Skyscrapers reach past the historic
Water Tower like fingers to the sky.

Lakefront Joggers enjoy the
sunrise in front of the newly
redesigned Adler Planetarium .

"There can be no better place than this.
There just can't."

Lori Garza -
Export coordinator

Gateway to the suburbs: Northwestern Train Station

"CHICAGO IS BEAUTIFUL.
PICTURES DON'T LIE."

KIMBERLY GOW
UNIVERSITY STUDENT

Since it was such a clear day, I rented a Limosine to take a tour of the city. Our driver from Metropolitan picked the six of us up at our hotel and suggested we start at the Sears Tower Skydeck. From there we could pick a direction in which to go.

Once at the top, my eldest son, Anders, tried his eight power binoculars and saw a large shopping center to the west. When we came down from the clouds, we asked our driver what Anders could have seen. He told us it was the Oakbrook Shopping Center.

We decided to go there and we enjoyed some great shopping. (We sure did! We packed the trunk!) We decided to have a late lunch and our driver suggested Tuscany Restaraunt in Oakbrook. Tuscany appeared to be a favorite place for the ladies to end their shopping

DAY. SHOPPERS COME FROM ALL THE SURROUNDING SUBURBS LIKE HINSDALE,

WHEATON, WINFIELD AND ELMHURST, AND NEARBY STATES.

WE ENJOYED STINCO DI VITELLA OSSOBUCO (SHANK OF VEAL WITH VEGETABLES)

AND SPAGHETTINI ALL' AMATRICIANA (HOMEMADE PANCETTA, SAUTEED ONION,

TOMATO SAUCE AND PARMIGIANO CHEESE). MY DAUGHTERS HAD THE GRILLED

VEAL CHOPS AND POLLO AL VESUVIO (1/2 CHICKEN SAUTEED WITH GARLIC, ROSEMARY AND WHITE WINE). WE SPOKE

TO SALVATORE FROM CALABRIA, WHO HAD RECENTLY VISITED OUR

HOMELAND. "WHAT A GREAT RESTAURANT!"

FRANZ OCHERMANN FAMILY,
BANKER, SAAS FEE SWITZERLAND

FOURTEEN TWENTY-FIVE WEST TWENTY-SECOND STREET

"Chicago has all the advantages of a big city and all the charm of a small town. That is the best of both worlds, and this is the best of all cities.

Joan Esposito
TV Newsperson

Marina City

BURNHAM HARBOR AT SUNSET

"CHICAGO IS SO MANY THINGS. IT IS
A HARBOR, A PARK, BIG BUILDINGS ....
AND HOT-DOGS!"

GEORG GARKUS
CAB DRIVER
RUSSIA

AN EXCLUSIVE EXPERIENCE

Metropolitan Limousine has earned the confidence of our clients by not only meeting their needs, but anticipating them. Attention to detail is second to none. We specialize in corporate service and your confidentiality is always assured. We understand that we may well be a first contact for you or your client. Therefore, all airport arrivals are met at the gate. We'll handle your luggage and take you to your waiting limousine. It's a superb way to arrive - smoothly. But, wherever we collect you, please be assured that a discreet, polite and professional member of our organization will be there to cater to your every need.

ENJOY CHICAGO IN STYLE

A number of our chauffeurs are available to offer personalized sightseeing tours. We believe it's a magnificent way to see Chicago and tours can be tailored to suit your time constraints and specific sights of interest.

AWARD WINNING SERVICE

Over twenty five years ago Metropolitan Limousine was founded on the premise of providing an exclusive and impeccable limousine service. A significant factor in our success is the professionalism and dedication of the Metropolitan chauffeurs. These attributes have not only been recognized by our clients - but by the National Limousine Association who have

AN IMPE
CHAUFFEU

awarded us "Operator of the Year" and "Chauffeur of the Year" four times in the past five years.

A FLEET TO SERVICE ALL YOUR NEEDS

Our fleet includes Mercedes, Town Car Sedans, extended Lincoln Limousines, passenger vans and motor coaches. Our vehicles are immaculate and all cars have direct dial mobile telephones. The fleet size and location allow us to cater to any of your last minute needs. Each car has a private, sophisticated radio system allowing the driver to communicate to our operations office. The flight arrival and departure information as viewed on airport monitors is broadcast live into our operations office.

NATIONAL AND INTERNATIONAL ATTENTION

Metropolitan Limousine is honored to be part of Dav-El's Worldwide Limousine Network. Fortune magazine correctly described us as "the largest limousine service...with offices everywhere." The system has offices in New York, Los Angeles, Washington D.C., Boston and Philadelphia, with affiliates in nearly every major U.S., Canadian and European city.

Metropolitan Limousine

845 North Michigan Avenue Chicago, Illinois 60611-2290
(312) 808-8000 (800) 437-1700
Group Sales Department: (312) 808-8883
limos@metropolitianlimo.com
www.metropolitianlimo.com

CCABLE R SERVICE.

IT WAS ONE OF THOSE CRAZY WEEKNIGHTS WHEN THE BEST LAID PLANS OF MICE AND DATEBOOKS OFT GO ASTRAY. I HAD PLANNED TO MEET FRIENDS IN CHICAGO'S OLD TOWN NEIGHBORHOOD. JUST AS I WAS TO LEAVE, THEY CALLED. TWO FRIENDS OF THEIRS WERE IN FROM THE PHILIPPINES. WHERE COULD WE GO FOR DINNER? I TOLD THEM I WOULD THINK OF SOMETHING. AS I CHANGED INTO SOMETHING MORE RELAXED, I HAD THE ANSWER. IT WAS RIGHT THERE IN THE HEART OF THE NEIGHBORHOOD.

AFTER WE WATCHED THE SUNSET FROM THE SEARS SKYDECK, WE THEN HEADED TO THE FIREPLACE INN AT 1448 N. WELLS IN OLD TOWN. FOR OVER 30 YEARS THIS RESTAURANT HAS DEVOTED ITSELF TO SERVING THE BEST BARBECUE RIBS IN THE CITY. AND THERE'S SEAFOOD. IN FACT, THAT MADE CHOOSING A LITTLE DIFFICULT FOR MY FRIENDS. THE COMBOS LIKE RIBS AND SHRIMP OR RIBS AND CRAB SATISFIED THE UNDECIDED ONES. I WENT STRAIGHT FOR THE RIB COMBO. BARBECUE HEAVEN WAS HERE ON EARTH WITH CHICKEN AND RIBS.

IN THE FIREPLACE INN'S SKI-LODGE ATMOSPHERE, WITH STAINED GLASS

AND OUTDOOR GARDEN, I FORGOT THE EARLIER CRAZINESS AND RELAXED. LATER, WE MOVED TO HOBOS,

A LITTLE CELLAR RIGHT NEXT DOOR. WE ENJOYED GREAT CONVERSATION OVER SEVERAL RACKS OF POOL

AND AFTER-DINNER DRINKS. THERE WAS ALSO A HUGE COLLECTION OF BOOKS AND FIVE TELEVISIONS WITH

NOTHING BUT SPORTS.

FOURTEEN FORTY-EIGHT NORTH WELLS STREET

WE CLOSED THE EVENING WITH WALK THROUGH THE LAMP LIGHT OF OLD TOWN. HORSE DRAWN

CARRIAGES CLOPPED THROUGH THE TURN OF THE CENTURY STREETS, LINED WITH ART GALLERIES AND

THEATERS. A STOP AT THE UP/DOWN TOBACCO SHOP TO PICK UP MY FAVORITE OLD MAID TOBACCO GAVE

MY FRIENDS A CHANCE TO SELECT SOME FINE CIGARS.

IN A SOCIAL EMERGENCY, I TOSS THE DATEBOOK OUT THE WINDOW AND CALL THE FIREPLACE INN AT

(312) 664-5264 AND THEY DELIVER MY SALVATION.

NORMAN ROSS
TV PERSONALITY

A CIRCLE OF ELEVATED TRAIN LINES FORMS THE FAMOUS LOOP THAT

CONNECTS WITH A MODERN TRANSPORTATION SYSTEM REACHING ALL

PARTS OF THE CITY AND SUBURBS INCLUDING TWO MAJOR AIRPORTS.

PROFESSIONAL TEAMS IN EVERY
MAJOR SPORT EXCITE FANS IN
MODERN VENUES THROUGHOUT
THE CITY. THE CHICAGO BEARS
DO BATTLE ON THE GRID-IRON
AT SOLDIER FIELD. THE
CHICAGO BULLS BASKETBALL
TEAM SHARES THE UNITED
CENTER WITH HOCKEY'S
CHICAGO BLACKHAWKS.

Chicago loves the national pastime so much that one baseball team is not enough.

The Chicago Cubs and White Sox play day and night games throughout the summer.

Both ballparks are located minutes away by elevated train or bus from the Loop.

DEDICATED FANS ARE NOT JUST
SPECTATORS, THEY ARE PART OF
THE SHOW AT WRIGLEY FIELD
AND COMISKEY PARK.

"ALRIGHT NOW, LET ME HEAR YA"!

THANKS, HARRY

SAMMY SOSA HITS NUMBER 56 ON HIS WAY TO A RECORD 66 HOME RUNS. "CHICAGO, I LOVE YOU."

THIRTY-SEVEN HUNDRED NORTH CLARK STREET

WE VISITED CHICAGO TO SEE OUR BASEBALL TEAM BATTLE THE CHICAGO CUBS FOR A WEEKEND SERIES. WE CABBED OVER TO WRIGLEYVILLE EARLY, SO WE WOULD HAVE TIME TO SEE THIS INTERESTING NEIGHBORHOOD BEFORE THE GAME. A STONE'S THROW (OR SHOULD I SAY, A HOME RUN) FROM THE BALL PARK IS TUSCANY ON CLARK, (773)-404-7700 AT THE CORNER OF CLARK AND WAVELAND. THE HOSTESS SEATING US NOTICED OUR CARDINAL JACKETS AND GAVE US A RUN-DOWN OF HOW OUR PLAYERS MIGHT DO AGAINST THE CUBS. NOT SURPRISING IN A NEIGHBORHOOD NAMED AFTER A BALL PARK.

SURROUNDED BY WINE BOTTLES AND ITALIAN CERAMICS, OUR TABLE WAS FUN AND FESTIVE WITH DISHES LIKE SPAGHETTINI ALA MARCELLINO (PASTA WITH GARLIC, OLIVE OIL, SHRIMP, SCALLOPS, FRESH SPINACH AND ROASTED PEPPERS) AND PETTICHI POLLO ALLA VALDOSTANA (CHICKEN BREAST STUFFED WITH PROSCIUTTO AND FONTINA CHEESE IN A SPECIAL WINE SAUCE).

As we dined on the outdoor patio, we saw fans buying

pennants, baseball caps and numbered jerseys of their

favorite players. I reminisced about seeing the Cubs play the

Tigers in the World Series as a boy. We then strolled across

the street to the classic Wrigley Field and watched an

exciting game under the lights, cooled by a wonderful lake

breeze.

Mr. and Mrs. Harry Sullivan,
Consultant- retired, St. Louis, Missouri.

Four major marinas, serving both power and sailing craft, line Chicago's Lakefront

A lucky couple may even have Lake Michigan all to themselves.

THE LAKE WILL REMAIN.

THROUGH A MIRACLE OF

ENGINEERING AND THE

DEVOTION OF THE CITY, THE

LAKE STAYS PRISTINE, TOUCHED

ONLY BY THE BOATS WHO SAIL IT

AND SWIMMERS WHO COOL OFF

IN IT.

FOURTY-SEVEN THIRTY-TWO NORTH LINCOLN AVENUE

I NEVER LET MORE THAN A FEW MONTHS GO BY WITHOUT A PILGRIMAGE TO THE "OLD NEIGHBORHOOD" AT

LINCOLN SQUARE. I RECENTLY TOOK THE FAMILY BACK TO THE INTERSECTION OF LINCOLN, LAWRENCE AND

WESTERN AVENUES, WHICH STILL ECHOES OF THE OLD WORLD. A SHORT RIDE NORTH FROM THE SEARS TOWER

ARE SIDEWALK CAFÉS, WITH PEOPLE ENJOYING COFFEE AND PASTRIES. THE STEADY STREAM OF SHOPPERS LEAVING

MEYER'S DELICATESSEN WITH GERMAN MEATS, BREADS AND OTHER DELICACIES REMINDS ME OF MUNICH.

IT DOES NOT GET ANY MORE GERMAN THAN THE CHICAGO BRAUHAUS, OUR GOAL FOR A LONG, LEISURELY

LUNCH. HARRY AND GUENTER KEMPF HAVE MADE THE

BRAUHAUS A FAVORITE FOR LOCALS AND VISITORS; A PLACE FOR

RELAXATION AND UNMATCHED MEALS. HARRY GREETED US AS

ALWAYS, BUT SOON DISAPPEARED INTO THE KITCHEN TO CREATE

TRADITIONAL DISHES INCLUDING WIENER SCHNITZEL, ROULADE,

ROAST DUCKLING, RED CABBAGE AND SAUERKRAUT. WE STARTED OFF WITH LARGE STEINS FILLED WITH ONE OF THE MANY IMPORTED BEERS IN THIS BAVARIAN ATMOSPHERE. BEFORE LONG THE TABLE WAS CROWDED WITH ORDERS OF PORK SCHNITZEL, KASSLER RIPPCHEN, AND BOILED PORK SHANK WHILE THE MUSIC PLAYED ON. BUT WE STILL HAD ROOM FOR APPLE STRUDEL WITH WHIPPED CREAM AND PLUM KUCHEN. I EVEN LEARNED A NEW WORD: AUSGEZEICHNET! EXCELLENT!

WE LOVE TO COME DOWN ON SUMMER NIGHTS FOR ONE OF THE FESTIVALS ON LINCOLN PLAZA AND ENJOY THE BRATWURST FROM THE BRAUHAUS JUST ACROSS THE STREET. NATURALLY, WE WOULDN'T MISS OKTOBERFEST. A CALL TO (773) 784-4444 GETS US RESERVATIONS FOR THE CHRISTMAS CELEBRATIONS WITH SINGING GROUPS IN COLORFUL COSTUMES AND EUROPEAN DECORATIONS FROM THE LOCAL SCHOOLS. EVERY NIGHT THERE IS DANCING AS GUENTER AND HARRY DELIGHT THEIR PATRONS WITH GERMAN FAVORITES.

IT WON'T BE LONG 'TIL WE'RE BACK.

THE HALL FAMILY,
PARK RIDGE, ILLINOIS

O'HARE INTERNATIONAL AIRPORT, HOME OF UNITED AIRLINES 1-800-241-6522 AND HILTON CHICAGO O'HARE 1-800-HILTONS

THROUGHOUT THE TWENTIETH CENTURY, CHICAGO HAS NEVER RELINQUISHED ITS CROWN AS A

TRANSPORTATION HUB. AS AIR TRAVEL REPLACED TRAINS AS THE CHIEF MODE OF TRANSPORTATION, THE

CITY EXPANDED WESTWARD, TAKING OVER AN OLD MILITARY AIRFIELD AFTER WORLD WAR II IN A FAR-

SIGHTED MOVE. THE AIRPORT'S DESIGNATOR, ORD, COMES FROM ITS ORIGINAL NAME: ORCHARD PLACE, BUT

THE FIELD WAS SOON RENAMED TO HONOR LIEUTENANT COMMANDER EDWARD "BUTCH" O'HARE. O'HARE

WAS A NAVAL PILOT FROM CHICAGO WHO RECEIVED THE CONGRESSIONAL MEDAL OF HONOR FOR BRAVERY

AFTER BEING KILLED IN THE PACIFIC DURING THE WAR.

CHICAGO'S SPIRIT TO CONSTANTLY REMAKE ITSELF IS REFLECTED IN THE DEVELOPMENT OF THIS ULTRA-MODERN

FACILITY. IT LENGTHENED ITS RUNWAYS AS THE JET AGE DAWNED. IN THE 70'S, THE O'HARE HILTON HOTEL WAS BUILT AS A HAVEN FOR HARRIED TRAVELERS JUST STEPS FROM THE TERMINALS THROUGH UNDERGROUND TUNNELS. IN THE 80'S AND 90'S , O'HARE COMPLETELY RENOVATED ITS TERMINALS TO ACCOMMODATE THE SOARING PASSENGER RATES.

TODAY O'HARE FIELD IS STILL THE BUSIEST AIRPORT IN THE WORLD WITH OVER 70 MILLION PASSENGERS YEARLY TRAVELING TO AND FROM ALL CONTINENTS, ON MAJOR CARRIERS SUCH AS BRITISH AIRWAYS, AMERICAN, CATHAY PACIFIC, IBERIA AND ROYAL JORDANIAN AIR. IT ALSO IS A CARGO GATEWAY FOR TONS OF GOODS FOR EVERY CORNER OF THE GLOBE.

"It reminds me of the crown jewels in the tower of London. It sparkles and dazzles. Diamonds, rubies and emeralds laid out at your feet."

FRANKLIN KING
BOXING PROMOTER
LONDON

AS SOON AS WE WALKED IN THE DOOR I KNEW MANNY'S HAD CHARACTER. IT WAS POPULATED BY BUSINESSMEN FROM THE AREA JUST SOUTH OF DOWNTOWN. I STUDIED THE 45-FOOT MENU BOARD AS I SLID MY TRAY ALONG THE CAFETERIA STYLE COUNTER. I HAD NO IDEA WHAT TO PICK, BUT I KNEW THAT, WHATEVER I WOULD ASK FOR, I WOULD GET PLENTY OF IT.

MANNY'S DESERVES ITS STATUS AS AN EATING LANDMARK. FOR OVER 50 YEARS, 35 AT THIS LOCATION AT 1141 S. JEFFERSON STREET, CHICAGOANS HAVE BEEN COMING HERE TO EAT, NOT DINE ON SPRIGS AND TWIGS, BUT EAT. PLATES PILED HIGH WITH PASTRAMI, ROAST BEEF, THE BIGGEST AND BEST CORNED BEEF IN CHICAGO SERVED WITH A POTATO PANCAKE AND A MUST - LAKE SUPERIOR WHITEFISH CHASED BY CHEESECAKE AND PIES. YOU COME HERE TO GET UN-HUNGRY. KEN RASKIN, THE THIRD GENERATION OWNER, WILL SEE THAT YOU DO.

WE WERE SURROUNDED BY NOSTALGIA IN THIS RETRO-50'S DINER THAT IS THE NOON HOME OF THE NEIGHBORHOOD LOCALS. NEWSPAPER CLIPPINGS LINE THE WALLS, SHOWING A FAMILY BUSINESS GROWING BY KEEPING ITS FAMILY TRADITIONS. THEY USED TO HAVE A VAN THAT CIRCLED THE NEIGHBORHOOD MAKING DELIVERIES. IT NEVER CAME BACK EMPTY—IT PICKED UP CUSTOMERS FOR LUNCH. MANNY'S STILL DELIVERS. YOU CAN CALL (312) 939-2855 AND THEY'LL BRING IN LUNCH FOR A DOZEN OR A HUNDRED.

You'll find all the deli standards on the huge 45-foot menu board—pickled beets, marinated

cucumbers, Rueben sandwiches and gefilte fish. I decided not to bother reading it at all. I asked

my stomach what it wanted. It said a Rueben, chocolate phosphate and cheesecake. I got it.

When we were done, it said "thanks, Manny's".

Matt Greenstein, Publisher.
Downtown Chicago

"FROM THE TOP OF THE SEARS TOWER, ONE MIGHT BELIEVE THE STREETS ARE PAVED WITH GOLD."

PAUL COLLINS
DESIGNER

"VISITORS ARRIVE UNCERTAIN. THEY LEAVE
ENAMORED."

WALLY PHILIPS
RADIO PERSONALITY

THE FIELD MUSEUM OF NATURAL HISTORY
IS A CENTER OF ON-GOING RESEARCH INTO
DINOSAURS AND PREHISTORIC MAN.

Over the years, we have carefully selected several restaurants which have the style and menu that we like to include in our evenings, by ourselves or with friends, often after the theater or opera. We had just enjoyed a fabulous performance at the Lyric Opera House and planned to finish the evening at one of our favorites.

TSUNAMI MEANS "GREAT WAVE" IN JAPANESE, BUT IN CHICAGO IT MEANS AUTHENTIC JAPANESE CUISINE AT THE

TSUNAMI RESTAURANT. TSUNAMI BLENDS THE ENERGY OF MODERN JAPAN WITH ANCIENT TRADITIONS THAT

STRETCH OVER A THOUSAND YEARS.

THE UPSTAIRS SAKE LOUNGE WAS ELECTRIC WITH POST MODERN DECOR THAT STIMULATES CONVERSATION. OLD

FRIENDS RELATED THEIR EXCITEMENT OVER THE LATEST PLAY OR SYMPHONY THEY HAD ENJOYED. ONE OF OUR

GROUP MET A LADY HE HAD KNOWN ON AND OFF OVER THE YEARS. WE WEREN'T SURPRISED WHEN THEY FOUND

AN INTIMATE TABLE INSIDE AMONGST ANTIQUE ART WHILE WE MOVED OUTSIDE TO THE SIDEWALK CAFÉ.

TRADITIONS DEVELOPED OVER CENTURIES TO BRING OUT THE FLAVORS OF SUSHI AND SUSHIMI ARE ALIVE AND

RESPECTED HERE. OVER OUR APPETIZERS OF SHRIMP AND VEGETABLE TEMPURA, WE WATCHED THE CROWDS FROM

NEARBY RUSH STREET EBB AND FLOW LIKE A GREAT SEA. SUSHI AND SAKE WITH SESAME ESSENCE BEEF TENDERLOIN

WITH LOBSTER MASHED POTATO, SUGAR SNAP PEAS AND TERIYAKI SAUCE WERE CAREFULLY PREPARED BY EXPERT

CHEFS ALONG WITH SELECTIONS OF NIGIRI AND MAKI MONO. WE ALSO AVAILED OURSELVES OF TSUNAMI'S

EXTENSIVE WINE LIST - A RARITY IN JAPANESE RESTARUANTS.

TSUNAMI'S PHONE NUMBER, (312)642-9911, IS PERMANENTLY IN

OUR LIST OF PLACES WE ENJOY OFTEN. THEY OFFER A PURE

POINT OF VIEW OF JAPANESE FOOD, TEMPERED WITH JUST THE

RIGHT MIX OF WESTERN TASTES - THE BEST OF BOTH WORLDS.

MR. AND MRS. DAVID WRIGLEY,
RESTORATION ARCHITECT, LAKE FOREST, ILLINOIS

ELEVEN SIXTY NORTH DEARBORN STREET

"I've been traveling the world since the early Sixties when the only thing people thought about Chicago was "Al Capone Land". Now, it's not unusual to hear first-time visitors refer to Chicago as "that wonderful city by the lake". And why shouldn't they? Ours truly is a wonderful and proud city - it is very clean with a fabulous lakefront, numerous beautifully sculpted parks and distinctive architecture.

"We have a thriving business center, world-class restaurants and, most of all, a diverse cultural community with first-rate museums, the Chicago Symphony Orchestra, the Lyric Opera, an ever-growing theater community and world-class dance companies... and I haven't even gotten to our music scene, including our much envied jazz and blues clubs.

"We are not without our problems - what major cities these days are? But the difference is that we have the courage to confront our problems and strive to work them out. We are the finest example today of great ideas and great people. We call it... Chicagoland!"

Ramsey E. Lewis Jr.

CHICAGO WILL REMAIN DEDICATED TO PEOPLE.

THOSE WHO LIVE HERE AND THOSE WHO VISIT WILL

ALWAYS BE ABLE TO PLAY OR WORK HERE AND TO

FIND HEART POUNDING EXCITEMENT OR QUIET

SOLITUDE.

ROMANTIC WALK: THE "GOLDEN COLLAR" NEAR LAKE SHORE DRIVE.

THE CHICAGO OF STONE AND
STEEL WILL NOT REMAIN FIXED
FOREVER. THE SEEDS OF THE
CITY'S FUTURE ARE SOWN
EVERYDAY. THE SKYLINE SEEMS
TO CHANGE MONTHLY AS
CONSTRUCTION CRANES
PIROUETTE TO A CONSTANT,
DRIVING THEME. DARING
DESIGNS ARC TO THE CLOUDS
AND ARE FILLED WITH PEOPLE
WITH NEW IDEAS AND VISIONS.

"I LOVE SEEING CHICAGO CHANGE TO MORE
BEAUTIFUL ARCHITECTURE EACH VISIT."

DANIEL BEEDERMAN
ATTORNEY

Four of us took the train in from Birmingham, Michigan. It always gives me a thrill to arrive at Union Station with its dramatic neo classical interior. Not many people know that Chicago is still a major rail hub.

During the roughly six hour trip in first class accomodations, we watched the Midwest roll by. We arrived in Chicago rested and eager to start our list of places to visit in town. Our friend, Mike picked us up and called (312) 266-0616 and 10 minutes later we were seated at Lino's Restaurant.

Our table was surrounded by the beautiful art and photographs of Italy, especially Florence. The wine was a perfect complement to dishes like Vitella Valdostana, (stuffed Veal Chop), Tagliata di Manzo ai Ferri (16oz. New York Steak slice, with fresh Garlic and Rosemary) and Pesce al Sale (whole fish of the day baked in a crust of salt).

TWO TWENTY-TWO WEST ONTARIO STREET

Everyone at Lino's made sure we enjoyed our meal. It was exciting to sample recipes

brought here from all over Italy.

After dinner, we walked a few blocks and topped the evening off singing at the Red Head

Piano bar until they closed. That's how we started our weekend!

Bill Wedell, Gymnastic Coach,
Rochester Hills, Michigan

We've just returned from an extended stay in Mexico. After celebrating New Years in Mexico City, we enjoyed Carnival in Veracruz. Then we had two short weeks photographing the pelicans and enjoying the winter sun in Mazatlán. In Puerto Vallarta we decided that we had a real love for Mexico.

On a double decker bus tour of Chicago, we passed the new statue of Juárez near the Wrigley Building. It reminded us that we hadn't had a real Mexican dinner in weeks. As the bus tour headed up Michigan Avenue, we decided to meet some friends at Salpicón in Old Town, about a mile from the Sears Tower.

Moments after arriving, we felt as if we were dining in someone's home in Mexico City. Salpicón is breath takingly decorated with paintings and ceramics. Our friends called (312) 988-7811 to see if we had arrived. As I answered the phone, they were pulling up in a Noble horse drawn carriage—complete with cellular phone.

Dinner was like reliving our stay in Mexico. Pollo en Mole Poblano, half of an Amish chicken was served in a classic Pueblan mole sauce with mexican rice for my wife and me. Our friends enjoyed their favorite: Seviche de Camarón y Pulpo con Aguacate, a spicy shrimp and octopus seviche marinated in orange and lime juices with habanero chiles.

We know we have found a portal back to Old Mexico that we can visit anytime we are in Chicago, so many dishes to try!

Richard Newberry, retired shoe store owner,
Pittsburgh, Pennsylvania.

THE HEART OF THE CITY IS NOT JUST STERILE STEEL AND GLASS. IT IS A

CONSTANT CELEBRATION OF THE SOUL OF THE CITY - PEOPLE.

PARADES, FESTIVALS AND MUSIC ARE ALL PART OF DAILY LIFE IN THE

FINANCIAL AND BUSINESS DISTRICTS OF THE "LOOP". EVEN AFTER

BUSINESS HOURS AND ON WEEKENDS PEOPLE STAY DOWNTOWN FOR

THEATERS, RESTAURANTS AND EVEN A RIDE IN A HORSE-DRAWN

CARRIAGE.

FIESTA ON STATE STREET

THE PEOPLE ARE THE FUTURE. THEY WILL CHANGE; NEW VISITORS AND CITY

DWELLERS WILL ARRIVE. THEY WILL LEAVE THEIR MARK IN SOME WAY THAT

WILL BECOME INEVITABLY CHICAGOAN. IN EXCHANGE THE "I WILL" SPIRIT

WILL GROW INTO EVERYTHING THEY DO OR DREAM.

ECHOES OF YESTERDAY

MICHIGAN AVENUE BRIDGE OVER THE CHICAGO RIVER

"IT'S LIKE A PILGRIMAGE. WE WAIT FOR THAT FIRST GREAT
DAY IN THE SPRING AND TAKE OUR BOATS TO THE BEAUTIFUL
LAKE. WHEN THE LAST BRIDGE GOES UP, WE'RE SET FREE."

DR. HAROLD ARAI
DENTIST
PARK RIDGE

"THE FIRECRACKERS! THE FOOD! I AM SO HAPPY WE WERE HERE FOR
CHINESE NEW YEAR IN CHINATOWN. ONLY SHANGHAI WOULD BE BETTER."

JAMES DEGUZMAN
FARMER
THE PHILIPPINES

"IT IS SO HARD TO IMAGINE WHAT HAS HAPPENED HERE. NOTHING BUT MARSHES AND GRASS. THEN CAME SETTLERS WITH TENTS AND SHACKS. AND THEN THE FIRE. I WISH THE PEOPLE STANDING IN THE ASHES COULD SEE THIS.... WHO KNOWS? SOMEHOW MAYBE THEY DID. AND THAT IS WHY THE CITY'S HERE."

BENJAMIN MILES
COWBOY
MINOT, NORTH DAKOTA

MERCHANDISE MART

MUSEUM OF SCIENCE AND INDUSTRY

"I HAVE TO COME BACK FOUR MORE TIMES. FIRST TIME I SAW JUST THE MUSEUMS. THERE IS SO MUCH IN JUST ONE OF THEM."

CHARLES FARINA
BOAT CAPTAIN
SARDINIA

FOURTEEN EIGHTEEN WEST FULLERTON PARKWAY

I'VE GOT TO SAY THIS IS ONE FAST MOVING CITY. YOU NEVER KNOW WHO YOU'LL MEET, RUB SHOULDERS WITH OR GET AN AUTOGRAPH FROM. ALL OVER THE LINCOLN PARK AREA, THEY'RE SHOOTING MOVIES AND TV SERIES. LAST TIME WE WERE IN TOWN, WE SAW MARK GRACE AND GOLDIE HAWN. AT STEFANI'S, A GREAT NEAR NORTH RESTAURANT, WE CAUGHT A GLIMPSE OF A MAN WITH A TRUE "FOLLOWING".

AFTER ENJOYING A DAY AT THE LINCOLN PARK ZOO, OUR CAB BROUGHT US OVER TO STEFANI'S ON FULLERTON. ARRIVING AT THE SAME TIME, A MAN WITH A CLERICAL COLLAR AND A BROAD SMILE WAVED TO SEVERAL PEOPLE. INSIDE THEY TOLD US HE WAS FRANCIS CARDINAL GEORGE, ARCHBISHOP OF CHICAGO. WE FIGURED IF STEFANI'S WAS GOOD ENOUGH FOR THE ARCHBISHOP, IT'S GOOD ENOUGH FOR US PROTESTANTS FROM BOSTON.

WE REALLY ENJOYED THE APPETIZER OF POLPI PICCANTINI ALLA GRIGLIA (GRILLED, MARINATED BABY OCTOPUS). WHILE WE DINED IN THEIR OUTDOOR GARDEN, SURROUNDED BY BEAUTIFUL FLOWERS AND FESTIVE ITALIAN MUSIC, WE ENJOYED OUR ENTREE OF FETTUCCINE AL SAPORE DI VERDURE, (GRILLED CHICKEN BREAST OVER FETTUCCINE WITH GRILLED VEGETABLE PESTO) AND A GLASS OR TWO OF LUNGORATTI ROBESCO, A FINE ITALIAN WINE.

THE OWNER, PHIL STEFANI, STOPPED BY PERSONALLY TO ASK HOW WE LIKED OUR FOOD AND SUGGESTED WE MIGHT CATCH A PLAY ON HALSTED STREET AFTER DINNER. I NEEDED A ROOM FOR AN UPCOMING

PHOTO VIC BIDER

CORPORATE MEETING, AND TOOK THE OPPORTUNITY TO ASK HIM ABOUT IT. A QUICK LOOK AROUND AND OUR DINNERS CONVINCED ME I NEEDED TO LOOK NO FURTHER. STEFANI'S HAS SEVERAL ROOMS FOR PRIVATE DINING OCCASIONS AND MEETINGS. I MADE A NOTE TO CALL HIM AT (773) 348-0111.

AFTER DINNER WE SAW A GREAT PLAY AT THE STEPPENWOLF THEATER, WHICH WE LAUGHED AT FOR TWO HOURS STRAIGHT! A MAGNIFICENT EVENING!

KEVIN MILFORD, ATTORNEY,
BOSTON, MASSACHUSETTS

CHICAGO'S HEART PULSES TO
THE BEAT OF MUSIC. BLUES,
GOSPEL, JAZZ, CLASSICAL AND
OPERA. ONE OF THE
BIRTHPLACES OF THE FABLED
ART, CHICAGO BOASTS BLUES
VENUES WITH STAR PERFORMERS
SIDE BY SIDE WITH UP-AND-
COMING MUSICIANS.
THE LYRIC OPERA AND
CHICAGO SYMPHONY
ORCHESTRA ARE HOMES TO
A WIDE RANGE OF TALENTED
ARTISTS. MUSIC FESTIVALS
FOR EVERY TASTE SPAN THE
ENTIRE YEAR.

"CHICAGO WRITES ITS OWN MUSIC. IT MOVES
TO ITS OWN BEAT AND GETS INTO YOUR
SOUL."

BOB HALE
CHICAGO BROADCASTER

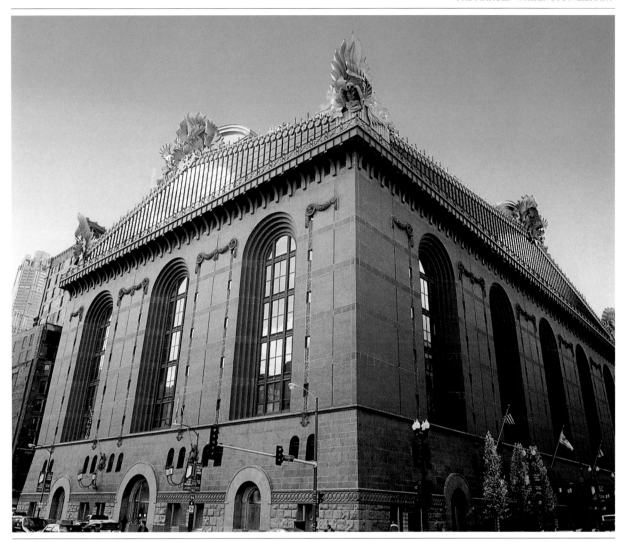

THE CITY'S MIND HAS ITS NEEDS, TOO. IN THE AFTERMATH OF THE GREAT CHICAGO FIRE OF 1871, AN ENGLISHMAN,

THOMAS HUGHES, ORGANIZED THE DONATION OF 8,000 BOOKS TO THE CITY. THE DONATIONS INCLUDED GIFTS

FROM QUEEN VICTORIA, BENJAMIN DISRAELI, ALFRED LORD TENNYSON AND ROBERT BROWNING. THEY SEEDED

A COLLECTION THAT BECAME THE MILLIONS OF VOLUMES NOW IN THE CHICAGO PUBLIC LIBRARY'S 78 LOCATIONS.

ACCLAIMED FOR ITS DARING NEO-CLASSICAL ARCHITECTURE, THE ANCHOR HAROLD

WASHINGTON LIBRARY CENTER AT 400 S. STATE STREET, IS ONE OF THE

FOREMOST EDUCATIONAL AND CULTURAL RESOURCES IN CHICAGO.

"MONUMENT WITH STANDING BEAST"
BY JEAN DUBUFFET
AT STATE OF ILLINOIS BUILDING

"WHY DO THEY MAKE THE RIVER GREEN
AND WHO WAS THIS SAINT PATRICK?"

DR. J. HARRANI
MALDIVES

"THE BRIDGES ARE AMAZING! THEY ALL
SWING UP LIKE SWANS RAISING THEIR NECKS
TO SALUTE THE BOATS."

MARTHA THYLIN
PHARMACIST
STOCKHOLM

Lake Michigan: Pristine waters for swimming and boating

AND THERE WILL ALWAYS BE THE PARKS AND THE DESIGN OF A

CITY IN A GARDEN. THEY WILL IMPROVE AND CHANGE TO FIT

NEW LIFESTYLES AND PEOPLES.

"There is one thing about Chicago that is constant. Change. The City seems always eager to grow and outdo itself. Restless, it greets the dawn everyday with its eyes looking upward. Bigger, better, faster. It seems sometimes the energy spills over into the electrical storms that light up the sky here. In the song the city is called "toddling". Children toddle. Chicago is a large zesty youth. Its toddling days are over."

MARYLIN MOONEY
UNITED KINGDOM

"In one word.... BOOM! Like a rocket. That's what I think of Chicago."

JOHN LEEMAN
FISHERMAN
NOVA SCOTIA

"I WAS SURPRISED YOU COULD SWIM HERE.
NOT A HUNDRED METERS FROM A HUGE CITY
AND I STAND IN PURE, CLEAN WATER."

VINCENT FARCHIE
SOCCER PLAYER
BOLOGNA, ITALY

OAK STREET BEACH

"AT THE SHEDD AQUARIUM, THEY HAVE A
FOREST ... INSIDE A BUILDING! IT IS BRILLIANT,
JUST HOW IT BLENDS RIGHT INTO THE VIEW
OF THE LAKE."

MICHAEL BARTLEY
JAVELIN THROWER
CLIFFS OF MOHR, IRELAND

SHEDD AQUARIUM

I LOST MY SUITCASE AND HAD BUSINESS AT
THE MERCHANDISE MART. FORTUNATELY,
THE A&G CLOTHING STORE IN THE MART
HAD A GREAT SELECTION OF EUROPEAN
DESIGNS. I CALLED HOWARD GOLDBERG AT
(312) 245-0377 AND THANKED HIM FOR
ALL HIS HELP.

ANTONIO LAZZARI
ROME

VIEW INTO THE "LOOP" FROM THE WEST

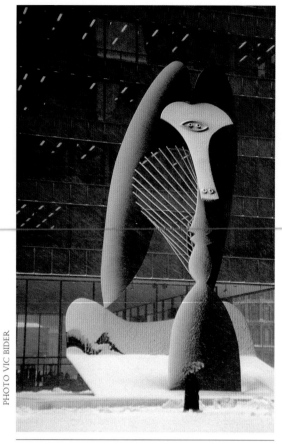

IT WAS A QUIET WINTER DAY WHEN I PASSED THE PICASSO SCULPTURE IN THE DALEY CIVIC CENTER PLAZA FOR PROBABLY THE THOUSANDTH TIME. SINCE ITS ARRIVAL IN 1967, THE ENIGMATIC PIECE HAS CHARMED CHICAGOANS AND ADDED TO THE WONDERFUL COLLECTION OF PUBLIC ARTWORKS THAT GRACE THE LOOP. IT IS SUCH A FAMILIAR OBJECT NOW, BUT IT STILL HELD A CERTAIN MYSTERY. SOMETIMES TO REALLY UNDERSTAND A WORK, IT HELPS TO SEE THE ENVIRONMENT WHICH SHAPED THE ARTIST.

IBERIA AIRLINES AND THE SPANISH TOURIST OFFICE IN CHICAGO GUIDED ME TO THE COSTA DEL SOL, THE SUN COAST. I FOUND IT WAS PERFECTLY NAMED. WEATHER GEOGRAPHY AND HISTORY HAVE ALL CONSPIRED TO CREATE A PARADISE OF MOORISH MYSTIQUE, MIXED WITH SPANISH SPICE, ALONG THE MARBELLA - MÁLAGA COAST. BASING MYSELF AT THE GRAN MELIA DON PEPE HOTEL IN MARBELLA, I SET OUT TO DISCOVER WHAT COULD HAVE INSPIRED THE MASTER.

FLOWERS DRAPING IRON-RAILED BALCONIES CONTRAST WHITE-WASHED BUILDINGS IN MARBELLA'S OLD CITY OF NARROW WINDING STREETS. I DISCOVERED A WONDERFUL SPANISH TRADITION, TAPAS, IN THE RESTAURANTE SANTIAGO, LOCATED IN THE PASEO MARTÍMO IN MARBELLA. OWNER SANTIAGO DOMINGEZ WAS A CULINARY TOUR GUIDE,

TAKING ME THROUGH A SEVEN COURSE ANDALUSIAN FEAST OF DORADA

A LA ESPALDA, A SEA BASS SPECIALTY.

THE MOORS AND ROMANS LEFT THEIR INDELIBLE MARKS ON THIS

CROSSROADS BETWEEN EAST AND WEST. A MOORISH CASTLE WAS THE HEART

OF MARBELLA. ROMAN RUINS WITH MOSAICS AND OTHER ARTIFACTS DOT

THE SURROUNDING LAND NEAR RONDA.

BUT IT WAS THE ENERGY OF THE PEOPLE THAT MOST IMPRESSED ME. THEY

CELEBRATE LIFE AND GIFTS OF NATURE WITH FESTIVALS AND FIESTAS IN MIJAS

AND OTHER TOWNS AROUND MARBELLA. I COULD SEE AND HEAR THIS ENERGY

DAILY IN THE PASSION AND THUNDER OF THE FLAMENCO DANCE AT CAFÉ DE

CHINITAS IN MADRID. I WONDERED IF PICASSO MIGHT HAVE BEEN AS MOVED

AS I WAS.

WHILE IN MADRID, I WANTED TO VISIT THE FAMED MUSEO DEL PRADO. JUST

STEPS FROM MY ROOMS AT THE VILLA REAL HOTEL I FOUND THE WORKS OF

GOYA, VASQUEZ AND, OF COURSE, PICASSO. MORE HISTORY I FOUND AT THE

BOTIN, A 250 YEAR-OLD REASTARAUNT WHERE THE FOOD IS COOKED IN THE

SAME WAY AS WHEN THE MOSAIC WALLS AND BEAMED CEILINGS WERE NEW.

BACK IN CHICAGO I QUICKLY BEGAN TO MISS SPAIN. I FOUND A PIECE OF

IT NOT FAR AWAY, JUST NORTH AT 739 N. LA SALLE STREET, I FOUND

AN OASIS OF SPANISH FOOD AND CULTURE AT IBERICO, A RESTAURANT

"It looks like my wife."

JACK VON BURING
CONSTRUCTION COMPANY OWNER
WORMS, GERMANY

"Beautiful? I do not know. It is like a
fountain of steel."

SILVIA MENDOZA
CANDLEMAKER
MEXICO CITY

"Picasso , Miro, Chagall.... Chicago is
a museum of art! The whole city!"

PENELOPE MEVRELOS
NURSE
ATHENS, GREECE

FAMOUS FOR ITS TAPAS.

TAPAS IS MORE THAN A TYPE OF CUISINE; IT IS A WARM ATMOSPHERE OF FRIENDS AND CONVERSATION THAT SURROUNDS THESE SMALL PORTIONS, SERVED WITH WINE, BEER OR, ESPECIALLY, SANGRIA. I WAS TAKEN BY THE VARIETY OF DELICIOUS FOODS, ESPECIALLY GAMPAS AL AJILLO (GRILLED SHRIMP WITH GARLIC SAUCE), THAT SEEMED TO BE FULL OF THE ENERGY OF SPAIN, SERVED IN SUCH A WAY SO THAT FRIENDS CAN ENJOY EACH OTHER'S COMPANY AS WELL AS THE MEAL.

IBERICO'S OWNER, JOSE LAGOA, FAITHFULLY IMPORTS MANY OF THE INGREDIENTS, COMPLETE WITH THEIR TRADITION. GRILLED CALAMARI, BAKED GOAT CHEESE IN TOMATO SAUCE, OCTOPUS AND SHRIMP, SEASONED WITH IMPORTED SPICES, OILS AND OLIVES DIRECT FROM SPAIN INSTANTLY TRANSPORT YOU THERE. THERE'S EVEN LIVE SPANISH TV. PATRONS ENJOY FLAMENCO DANCERS AND SOCCER DIRECT FROM THE OLD WORLD. I WAS ONLY A LITTLE SURPRISED TO SEE PLACIDO DOMINGO ENJOYING AN EVENING WITH FRIENDS AT IBERICO.

I WENT BACK TO THE PICASSO AND SAW IT HAD CHANGED. IT WAS NOW PART SUN, PART SPICE AND ALL THE ENERGY I HAD FOUND IN THE MASTER'S HOMELAND.

PHOTOGRAPHER. DAVID MAENZA

"THEY DON'T CALL IT THE WINDY CITY
FOR NOTHING. BUT IF YOU DON'T LIKE
THE WEATHER IN CHICAGO, JUST WAIT
A MINUTE, IT'LL CHANGE."

UNKNOWN

PHOTO OF THE WRIGLEY BUILDING
FROM ROOSEVELT ROAD AND
SOUTH MICHIGAN AVENUE